A Sutton and Starr Mystery

MILLION-DOLLAR FRAUD

J.E. DUKE

Million-Dollar Fraud - A Sutton & Starr Mystery - (Book 3)

Copyright © 2017 H.A.R.P., Inc.

Digital ISBN #978-0-9993329-2-4
Print ISBN #978-0-9993329-3-1

Book layout by www.ebooklaunch.com

As always, to my family

Personal thanks to Charlee Liaromatis

A special MAHALO to Wilma Dela Cruz

CHAPTER 1

Offices of Sutton & Starr Private Investigators

Milo Starr was half-awake as he drove to the office. His partner, Jordan Sutton was half-asleep in the passenger seat. Milo was trying to revive himself after four very long stakeout nights. The unfaithful wife he had been tailing didn't return home until just before dawn. All he could think of was coffee as he yawned for the hundredth time and muttered to himself, "I wonder if it's Monday or Tuesday?"

He drove past their West L.A. office building, and as he did every morning, he glanced up at their amazing-looking sign that read, **"Sutton and Starr Private Investigators."** He looked over at the "Sutton" from the sign and saw that his partner was still sleeping and looked at peace with the world.

The car came to an abrupt stop in their parking garage, and Jordan opened her eyes. "Was I sleeping?" Milo laughed as he exited the car. "You always fall asleep, and you always ask the same question when you wake up." He set the car alarm, took his partner's arm

1

and guided her to the elevator. She pushed the button and leaned against the wall.

Milo yawned again but managed to say, "We have to move the office closer to the condo or move our condo closer to the office." Jordan looked confused. "We're not moving; we love our home. It's in a nice area, there's plenty of shopping, and there's you. You're there." Milo smiled and thanked her for the kind words but said, "Okay, we stay, but let's find a faster way to get here because L.A. freeway traffic keeps getting worse." The elevator doors opened, and Jordan wanted to know what she missed on the all-news radio station. "They were still yacking about the city-wide crime spree and the very talented private Investigators that solved everything." The elevator stopped on three. Milo stretched and ambled down the hallway to their office. Entering the small reception area, they expected to get a standard cheery greeting from their secretary, Carol, but instead, she had her head buried behind the morning newspaper and what they saw was a blaring headline.

"THE CRIMES OF THE CENTURY
THE FULL STORY"

Carol put down the paper and did give them a happy greeting. "Good morning. I was just reading about you two." Milo said he didn't have to read it; he lived it. Carol handed him the paper. "Well, you should read it because they paint you and Jordan as being L.A.'s version of Batman and Robin." Milo took the morning edition and started to leave. Carol looked at him and said, "Before you go, you want to explain all this new security stuff you had installed?" He told her he would explain everything, "After I snooze for a few minutes." Carol laughed, "Sorry, but you have a new client showing up in less than an hour."

Milo entered his office, and as he was closing the door, Carol yelled, "You should wash your face and shave. You look like you've been out all night." Milo mumbled, "That's why I look like this." Jordan was on the couch, looking fresh as a daisy as she read the paper. "I like the way they wrapped up the story. We really do sound like a mythical crime-fighting duo." Milo dragged himself into his small washroom. "That's why our phone has been ringing non-stop and why we've seen so many clients over the past few weeks."

He ran the electric razor over his face and splashed on some after-shave lotion. He emerged from the washroom with a smile. "Ta-Da! Do I look alive?" Jordan laughed, "Yes, you look like you're rested and ready to go." Milo plopped in his chair, turned on his computer, and his desktop opened with the day and date. He couldn't believe it. "It's Wednesday? The last day I remember was Saturday." He began to look over his email then stopped and buzzed Carol. "Have you been checking the email?" She cracked open his door, "Of course, I always look over the email and sort them. I have a call list for you. Do you want it now?" Milo told her he would read it after their early meeting. He closed the email program and looked over at Jordan calmly reading their story again. "You did very well on the last case. The crime scenes were very grizzly, and you took them all in stride." Jordan smiled, folded the paper nicely and approached his desk.

"Do you remember the first crime I was assigned to when I was a police officer?" He didn't. "No, ex-officer Sutton, I don't think you ever told me about that." Jordan smiled and leaned against his desk. "I was on the force all of two weeks and my training officer, Dirk Bolson heard about a murder in a sleazy hotel in downtown Los Angeles. He got us assigned there for crowd-control. The instant we walked into that crap hole and started up the creaking stairs, I could already smell the crime scene. The sickening odor was worse the closer we got to the room. There was a rotting corpse in the bathtub." Milo leaned forward and smiled, "Oh Lord! That sounds like a rookie's nightmare."

She smiled as she said, "Yes it was. We walked directly into that room, and as I approached the tub, it was all I could do to keep my breakfast down. Officer Bolson told me to look at everything in the bathroom and remember as much as I could. He said he'd ask questions later. I looked and gagged, but I didn't throw up. I knew if I did, I would have been the laughingstock of the department and I would never have lived it down. The body was so badly decomposed that I couldn't have told anybody if it was a man or a woman." Milo was smiling as he listened to his beautiful partner.

"The hotel room was a mess. Blood everywhere from what looked like a massive fight. My training officer saw that I was getting green around the gills, so we left the room and went into the hall. He told me to stay there and guard the room until the CSI unit got there." Milo loved the story. "Did you stay?" She nodded, "Yes. I opened a window in the hall for air, but that didn't help. I stood outside that horrible place for at least an hour while Officer Bolson was down in the street eating hot dogs off a cart. I'll never forget that event or that smell. It was horrid."

Milo asked if she got good marks for that day. "Yes, but Bolson said I really stunk. I needed a shower ASAP, and he told me to burn my uniform and shoes. He held his nose as we drove back to the precinct. So, the mutilation murder scenes of the so-called Crimes of the Century were similar. But for me, they were nothing I hadn't seen or smelled before." Jordan stopped and listened as Milo said, "No wonder the two-hundred-fifty plus crime scenes we had to visit didn't bother you." Their quiet moment was interrupted by Carol's buzz. *"Your next appointment is here."* Milo smiled and stood to welcome the possible new client.

Milo and Jordan both shook hands with the very attractive lady wearing a stylish cream-colored designer suit. She had an elegant air about her. Jordan smiled and motioned toward the chairs. Sutton and Starr looked at their guest and waited to hear what she needed. "I'm Ellen Davis. I called you about a problem I'm having with my husband." "Welcome, Mrs. Davis, what can we do for you?" She paused and looked at Jordan.

"I believe my husband Bradley is currently seeing two or three other women." She paused and looked directly at Milo. "I would like to hire your firm to follow him and find out what he's doing." She opened her handbag and placed a family photo on the desk. Milo looked at the picture and thought they were a very nice-looking group. The two adults and two children looked happy, but in this line of work, he knew all too well that smiles in front of the holiday tree might not be real. Over the past six years, he built his business on disgruntled marriage stakeouts. Milo passed the photo to Jordan and asked Mrs. Davis, "Is your husband out every night?"

Mrs. Davis adamantly shook her head, "No, he's home at night!" Jordan wondered why she thought her husband was fooling around. "Well, when I call him during the day he's never in the office. I just get his voice mail." Milo asked about his job. "He's an insurance agent. He's their top sales person and always seems to be out on client calls." Mrs. Davis stopped and then added, "When he returns home, he sometimes smells of perfume, and I've found lipstick on his clothes." Jordan was listening intently and wondered, "How do you know or think he's been with different women?" The wife looked at Jordan, "Different perfume scents and several lipstick shades on his shirts." Jordan had to turn toward Milo, so the client wouldn't see her smiling. Mrs. Davis asked, "May I speak with Ms. Sutton alone?" Milo replied, "Of course."

The ladies entered Jordan's office, and she listened as Mrs. Davis gave her a short lecture on how to tell if your husband was fooling around. Jordan understood because her story was almost identical. Her first and *only* husband was a player. The ladies returned about twenty minutes later, and Jordan announced that they had enough information.

"We'll be in touch." Mrs. Davis thanked them for their time. Milo watched her as she walked to the door. When they were alone, Milo asked, "Do we have a new client?" Jordan closed the door. "Yes, we do. Her story is about the same as mine. Her husband probably has multiple partners, and he doesn't have any interest in intimacy at home."

Milo was shocked at that statement. "How can you not want to have sex with that woman? She's really hot." Jordan quickly turned and glared at her partner/boyfriend. "What? I can't believe you said that in front of me." Milo was grinning from ear-to-ear. "I'm just messing with you. But you have to agree, right?" Jordan relaxed and really did have to agree with him. The lady was cute and had a terrific body. She wondered how they should proceed with the investigation. Milo thought for a moment, "It's a daytime surveillance for sure." Milo asked if she got all the contact information. "Yes, I have everything, so we can do a search on Bradley tonight and start to watch him tomorrow." Milo reached in his pocket for a coin. "I'll flip you for who gets to do the stakeout."

Carol popped in with a special package for Milo. "This was just hand-delivered by an FBI messenger and here's your list of calls." Milo put the coin back in his pocket and took the pouch. "This is what CR said he'd send over today." Inside they found an official FBI file folder marked:

"For Milo Starr and Jordan Sutton Only"

He turned the folder away from Carol who wanted to know what it was all about. He showed it to Jordan who looked at Carol. "It's a personal file from the FBI." Carol turned to exit the office, "I understand. You'll tell me later." Milo replied, "Don't know if we can." Carol smiled as she closed his door, "You know you will."

Milo laughed, "Yes, you know she's right." Jordan agreed. Milo grabbed his letter opener. Inside he found a note from their long-time FBI friend, CR Reid. He looked over the note then read it to Jordan.

"Milo and Jordan: My Section Chief wants to thank you for your help in solving the city-wide mutilation murders. He asked me to give him a total of the hours you spent working on the case. Milo, I know you don't keep track of such things, but I do. I noted every meeting, all the phone calls, and calculated your time spent at the crime scenes and on stakeouts. I presented the bureau an invoice for you. The enclosed check is payment for your involvement in the case. If it's not correct, let me know. CR"

Milo handed the note to Jordan and opened the enclosed envelope. He looked at the check and handed it to his partner who blurted out, "Eighty-five-thousand dollars? That's fantastic." Jordan put the check in her purse. "Let's drop by the bank on the way to dinner."

Milo agreed as he looked over his call list. "Do you know James Forbes?" Jordan thought for a moment but didn't know the guy. "He's emailed us several times in the past week, and he's on our call list, twice." Milo entered the foyer. "Carol, what did James Forbes say when he called?" Carol looked at her notepad. "He's called twice and really wants to talk to both of you. He didn't give me any details, but I got the impression it's important."

Milo thanked Carol and asked if they had anything else today. Carol replied, "No, that's it for today." Jordan with purse in-hand said, "Then we're out of here. Lock-up, I'll see you tomorrow. Mr. Starr will be out of the office following Bradley Davis. He lost the coin toss."

CHAPTER 2

The Stakeout

.Milo spent several hours after dinner searching for information about Bradley Davis. He didn't turn up anything negative on the husband. He found that Mr. Davis was an insurance agent who was number one in sales. He was also a member of his church choir and a Little League coach. Since Milo lost the coin toss and had to take the first watch on Mr. Davis who, according to his wife, had almost the same schedule every day. He would arrive at the insurance company just before nine o'clock, and then he was always out on sales appointments. Milo also returned a few calls from his list but had to leave a message for James Forbes. He shut down his computer system and joined Jordan in the bedroom. She was already asleep which was fortunate because he was too tired for another all-night session.

Early the next morning the P.I. parked across the street from Talbert Insurance and began the one thing he hated to do; sit and wait for something to happen. Milo called the insurance office to ask if he could meet with

Mr. Davis and was told that the agent would be out of the office most of the day. He checked in with Carol and asked if there was anything he needed to do. She said it was quiet around the office. "We're catching up on email and paperwork. You had a call from James Forbes. I told him you'd call back." Milo asked Carol to give his cell number to Mr. Forbes. "Maybe he'll call while I'm sitting here doing nothing." Jordan and Carol were really having some "girl time" in the empty office. Which meant they were talking about shoes and purses. Carol asked about the stakeout.

"So far, nothing. Can I talk to Jordan?" Carol looked, and Jordan was snoozing in Milo's super-soft chair. "She's on the phone right now. I'll tell her you called." Milo laughed and said, 'I'll bet you two are sitting around drinking coffee and talking about shoes and handbags." He disconnected the call and put more money in the parking meter.

The morning dragged on and there was nothing to report until just before twelve-thirty when Mr. Davis left the building, briefcase in hand. Milo sat up and stretched his arms as he watched the dark blue sedan pull out of the company's parking lot and head down the block. After letting one car proceed, Milo followed at a safe distance. The insurance agent didn't have far to go. He turned into a parking space next to a coffee shop about three blocks away. Milo was waiting in traffic to turn left into the parking lot. He watched as his well-dressed subject locked his car and entered the 50's retro-diner. Milo parked, went inside and took a seat not too far away from his target.

Mr. Davis greeted a young couple and Milo assumed it was an insurance presentation. He looked over the quaint menu and ordered a tuna sandwich and coffee from a waitress dressed in a pink and green uniform complete with a purple beehive hairdo. He was thinking *"this is a strange place for a business meeting."* But that's what was going on.

The insurance agent handed papers to the young couple who seemed barely twenty-one and was referring to the charts and graphs on his open laptop. He was conducting a full-on insurance sales presentation. Milo watched and made a few notes about his target: *Well-dressed, slight graying, slim & trim, very professional, ultra clean car.* Milo ate slowly and continued to glance over at the other table from time to time. He managed to snap a cell phone photo of the meeting while faking a call.

The couple must have liked what they heard because they signed on the dotted line. Mr. Davis continued to talk with his new clients for a few minutes. Milo heard what he thought was his phone ringing, but it was Mr. Davis who took a call. Milo realized he had the same ring-tone as Mr. Davis, as he put his phone back in his pocket. The insurance agent wrapped up the meeting, put the laptop and papers in his briefcase, paid the check and left the restaurant. Milo waited a few moments then followed him to the parking lot and watched as the blue sedan pulled out and headed in the opposite direction from the insurance office.

P.I. Starr, a very experienced detective, always followed his "mark" at a safe distance. Milo slowed and watched Mr. Davis pull into the parking area of Beautee Cosmetics. Milo parked in a spot across the street, under a large tree, and turned off his engine. He took a call from Jordan who wanted to know how his daytime stakeout was going. He gave her a quick rundown of his day so far including what he had for lunch. "Jordan, I can't get online from here, can you search for Beautee Cosmetics? Tell me what they do. Mr. Davis just stopped there, and it looks like he's on another sales call." Jordan asked if Milo saw any girlfriends yet. "No. So far, he's all business. Are you checking the company?" She put the phone on speaker and did a quick search. "It's a direct sales outfit. Their associates sell cosmetics and vitamins." Milo thanked her, "I'll see you in a while."

During the next hour, he saw a lot of ladies going and coming from the business. Milo was stretching and getting a bit tired of sitting and doing nothing when Mr. Davis exited the building, carrying what looked like a small, dark blue sample case. Milo started his car and watched as his target left the parking lot quickly and drove in the direction of the freeway. Milo had to wait for the traffic to clear so he could make a wide left turn. For a moment, he thought he'd lost the dark blue sedan but found it sort of hidden from view at a stop light behind a delivery van.

Milo followed Mr. Davis as he entered the freeway and stayed two cars behind him in the right lane. The insurance agent left the freeway just three exits later. Milo wondered if the guy knew he was being tailed. He slowed down as he followed the car down the freeway exit and got stopped at the bottom of the ramp by a traffic signal. Milo was tapping the steering wheel as he strained to look for the target car. As soon as the light was green, he sped away checking left and right for Mr. Davis. Down the road, about two blocks ahead, he caught a glimpse of the subject's car as it turned right off the main drag. He followed the blue sedan into a subdivision. The subject parked on the street and headed toward a home, carrying the small blue case.

Milo stopped, took a deep breath and parked down the block from his target's car. He retrieved his small binoculars from the glove compartment and used them to scan the house. It was in a very nice upscale area with two-story homes, manicured yards, and three-car garages. Except for Mr. Davis' car, the street was empty. A short time later, a car parked in front of the home. Several ladies were laughing as they exited the car and entered the house.

He relaxed for a moment, opened the driver's side window and started to play a game of Sudoku on his phone when it rang. The call was from James Forbes who wondered when Milo and Jordan could meet with him and his wife at their Beverly Hills office. Milo made a few notes and told Mr. Forbes, "I'll call as soon as I get back to my office. I don't have my schedule with me." Mr. Forbes thanked Milo and said he was looking forward to talking to them. Milo sat for another hour before the front door of the home opened and several women stepped onto the porch. They waited for Mr. Davis, who stopped and shook hands with each lady. Milo didn't know what to make of what he just saw, but he made a mental note and followed the blue sedan as it drove away.

The private eye followed Mr. Davis back to his insurance office and then he cut off the surveillance. Milo called Carol and said he would be in soon. He parked in his reserved space and didn't wait for the elevator. He rushed up the three flights of stairs because he couldn't wait to tell Jordan what he learned. He entered the office out of breath, with a gigantic smile on his face saying, "You're gonna love this!" He plopped down in his high-back chair and waited for Jordan and Carol to join him. They entered and saw that he was super excited about something.

Jordan was first to ask, "What's the matter?" He relaxed a bit and put a big smile on his face. "Nothing's the matter. I just want to tell you both about the stakeout. Ready?" He paused and continued to smile, "Mr. Davis not only sells insurance, but I think he might have a direct sales business too. I believe he sells cosmetics and perfumes. In my opinion, he's not having an affair." Jordan laughed very loud, "So, you think that's why he smells like perfume. I wonder why he never told his wife."

Milo continued, "I followed him from the insurance company to a sales lunch then he stopped at Beautee Cosmetics for a while. I continued to follow him to a home in a subdivision. He stayed there a little over an hour, and when he came out, six ladies said goodbye to him on the porch. I have to find out what was that all about." Carol chimed in, "Sounds like he was hosting a Beautee Cosmetics house party. I've been to several of those." Milo didn't know what she meant. Carol was delighted to explain. "A bunch of neighborhood people get together, and a representative comes and does product demonstrations. They give away samples, take orders and have door prizes. It's fun." Milo smiled and said, "Thanks, Carol. I guess that's what was happening. Let me get all my notes into the computer, and then we can get out of here." About an hour later he had everything entered and uploaded to his cloud server.

Carol asked about all the new security stuff they had installed. Milo gave her a quick overview of everything. "We had new glass installed in this office which makes it totally secure. Nobody can snoop on us. So, if you want to make a super private phone call, do it from here. We also have cameras rigged to the alarm system and panic buttons under each of our desks. They open an audio channel and contact the alarm company." Carol asked, "We need all of that, why?"

Jordan said, "Don't forget the sliding wall panel so we can hide the bulletin board. We deal with some very strange people, and it's nice to have this level of protection." Carol smiled at Jordan and glanced at Milo. "You're right; he *is* very strange sometimes." Milo laughed and checked his phone log. He called James Forbes, but he had to leave a message. *"Mr. Forbes, call me anytime on my cell phone."*

The alarm was set, and they all left the building at the same time. "Straight home for you Carol?" She entered her car and said, "Yes, I have a pot roast waiting for me. Hope you two have a nice evening." They waved as she drove away. Jordan opened the car door and asked, "What are we eating tonight?" Milo said, "I want to toss peanut shells on the floor."

Jordan knew that meant they weren't eating at the Ritz. They were going to one of their favorite local bars, Margo-Rita's. Jordan loved the place because it was illuminated by two dozen neon beer signs and every lady looks great in that type of lighting. Everyone was happy to see the "Private Dicks" as they called them. Margo asked, "With salt?" Jordan smiled, "Yes, two with salt for me, I don't know what the hell he wants." While they waited for their top-shelf Margaritas to arrive, Jordan wanted to hear about Milo's outing again, in detail.

Milo said it was a very routine operation. "I didn't see any girlfriends, but after what I did see, I don't think Mrs. Davis has anything to worry about." Margo delivered their drinks. "This one is strong; it's yours." She pushed that drink to Jordan. "This one is weak because you're driving." Milo raised his glass to their friend. "Thank you. You know what else I need?" Margo replied, "Yes, you need peanuts."

Milo laughed, "Yes, that's one thing I need, and I also need a driver, so I can drink when I go out at night." She pulled out her order pad, "Would you like to eat? We're serving chili dogs and onion rings. Is that ok?" Both Milo and Jordan said that would be great. On the way to the kitchen, Margo scooped up a bowl of peanuts and placed it on their table. Milo said, "Thank you! Now my evening is complete."

Jordan reached across the table and ran her perfect nails down Milo's arm. "Can't you think of anything that would make your evening even more complete?" Milo decided to mess around with his girlfriend's brain. "Let's see, booze, peanuts, and a chili dog. Nope, that's about it." Jordan slipped out of her shoe and put her warm foot in Milo's crotch. "Are you sure?" Milo smiled and raised his glass to her. "Okay, you got me. Sleeping with you tonight would really make my evening complete." Just as he said that Margo placed their dinners on the table. Milo loved every minute of the sensual under table massage, but he was turning red, so Jordan slipped back into her shoe.

It was a very messy, but relaxing dinner. The chili dogs were perfect, and the onion rings were even better. Jordan wiped some sauce from Milo's mouth as she asked if he was going to find out more about Mr. Davis and his second secret job. "Yes, I want to search the Beautee Cosmetics website and see if they list him. I think if we know what he does there, and we tell his wife, we might be able to help them repair their marriage." Milo paid the tab and said, "What do you think?" Jordan hugged her guy and whispered, "That's the kind of talk that makes me love you more." They waved to Margo who waved back and yelled. "See you soon. Don't be strangers."

As they drove, Milo thanked her for the surprise massage. "Do you remember the first time you did that to me?" Jordan thought about it but couldn't come up with an answer. "It was during our stay at the cute hotel by the sea, the place where we had our first encounter." Jordan suddenly remembered, "Yes. It was The Seaside Cottage Hotel." She looked at Milo, smiled and reached over to lightly touch his hand. "Thank you for bringing that up. That was a wonderful time for us. We should go back there again sometime."

When they got to the condo, Milo immediately started an Internet search trying to find information about Mr. Davis. Jordan took a nice long, singing shower and when she was finished, her partner was still at the computer. "Are you coming to bed?" Milo looked up and saw his beautiful roommate wearing only a bath towel and inviting him to the bedroom. He didn't have to be asked twice. He let the search continue, locked up the house and turned off the lights.

CHAPTER 3

Meet the Husband

Milo's day started about the same as many others. He showered, shaved, got his favorite dark roast coffee and tickled Jordan's toes to wake her. "What? What time is it?" Milo sang his answer, *"It's morning. Time to get up."* Jordan rolled over and said something into her pillow. Milo moved a little closer, "What did you say?" She rolled over a few inches and asked what he found with his search. "I was having such a good time with you last night that I forgot all about it. I'll look now."

He went directly to his computer and checked the results from his overnight search. "Wow, you gotta see this. Jordan, come look!" She wrapped her not-awake-self in the top sheet and slowly made her way to the couch. "Okay, what did you find?" Milo pointed to a section of the Beautee Cosmetics website. "Look who's here." She blinked her slightly blurry eyes. "Is that Bradley Davis?" Milo said, "Yes, except notice the name." She read the caption under the picture. "Bradley Baker, Leading Sales Consultant of the Quarter. Is that the same guy?"

Milo expanded the photo, "The picture is probably a few years old, but it's the same person. His bio says he outsells every other consultant. Mr. Davis or Baker is going to be speaking at their annual sales conference. His topic will be, *How to Make Every Customer Feel Special*." Jordan groaned, "I don't believe it. He isn't fooling around! You were right; he's just selling lipstick and perfume. That's why he goes home smelling like that." Milo printed out a few pages. "Yes, that's about it. How do you want to handle this?" Jordan sat up. "Me? Why me?"

Milo sat next to her on the couch and put his arm around her shoulders, "Because you had a quiet moment with the wife." Jordan reluctantly headed toward the bathroom and stopped. "Okay, but I don't know what to do." She did a short shower symphony and cracked the door. "How about this? I contact the cosmetic company and make an appointment with Mr. Davis ah...Baker and when he comes to the office, we tell him what's going on."

Milo liked the concept but had an additional idea. "How about we put his wife in your office, and after we tell him what's up, we bring her in. What do you think about that?" Jordan didn't love that idea. "Let's find out why he's working two jobs first and play it by ear from there." Milo agreed, and Jordan was all smiles as they headed toward the office. "Did I tell you I talked with James Forbes?" Jordan didn't know what he was talking about but stopped to listen. "He said he wants to hire us for a special job. We're supposed to meet him at his Beverly Hills office soon." Jordan shrugged her shoulders and said, "Okay, let me know when."

Carol greeted them with coffee and wanted to know what was in the FBI envelope. Milo wasn't talking. He just shook his head, no. Jordan thanked her for the coffee and went directly to her office to make the call to Beautee Cosmetics. Milo checked his email and was warming his hands on the coffee cup as Jordan entered. "I just called the cosmetics company and set up an appointment with Mr. Davis or rather Baker. He'll be here today at ten." Milo stopped pacing. "What about his wife? Are you calling her in too?"

Jordan sat in Milo's very plush chair. "No, I thought I'd talk to him first. I might get some free perfume too." Milo smiled, "That might work. Let's see what happens." Carol buzzed. *You have a call from James Forbes and Jordan has one from a cosmetic company.* Milo took his call and Jordan left to pick up hers. "Hi, this is Milo Starr." Mr. Forbes was all business as he explained that he and his wife had been following Sutton and Starr's exploits on social media and in print.

He wondered when they could meet at their office. "We need help with a situation that I can't mention over the phone." Milo checked his desk calendar and asked if they could meet the next morning. Mr. Forbes agreed and said he'd send all their contact information by email. Milo ended the call, checked more email and wandered into the lobby to tell Carol about their meeting tomorrow with James Forbes. He asked if Mr. Baker arrived. "Yes, he just got here. He and Jordan are in her office." Milo looked toward her closed door. "I wonder how she's doing." Milo was just returning to his office when Jordan stuck her head out of her door.

"Carol, come in for a moment, I want you to see this night cream." Carol smiled at Milo and said, "Sure, I'd love to."

Milo had no idea what was going on, but he figured Jordan had things under control. He smiled and headed back to his computer to check Mr. Forbes' internet presence. He found that Forbes and Associates was a CPA firm located in Beverly Hills that had been in business for six years. Mr. and Mrs. James Forbes were involved in many high society charity organizations and contributed to many worthy causes. About thirty minutes later Carol and Jordan said goodbye to their new cosmetics salesman and entered Milo's office smelling like perfume models. Milo asked, "How did it go?" Jordan said, "It was a nice first meeting. I tried to get him to make a pass at me, but he was all business." Carol thought it was fun. "He gave me some samples too. These are very nice products." Carol took her free stuff and went back to her desk. Milo wondered how Jordan wanted to proceed with the case. She wasn't sure. "I think we need to have a sit-down with the wife and then maybe get her and the hubby together."

"Just got an email from James Forbes and we have a meeting tomorrow at eleven at their office in Beverly Hills. I already told Carol. I'm going to finish up my call list and then let's get out of here for today. You smell like you should be on a date." Jordan liked that idea and asked where they were going? "I would like to throw peanut shells on the floor, but you look and smell too nice for that."

One hour later Milo was finished with everything and asked Jordan if she was ready. She didn't say a word;

she just took his arm and dragged him to the lobby. "Where are you going?" They looked at Carol and said, "We're going to lunch. Can we bring you something?" Carol pointed to her desk calendar. "You're not going out for at least an hour or more." They didn't understand. "You have a major interview with ES, The Entertainment Syndicate." Milo stopped, "You're right, I forgot all about that." Carol told him that she left a note on his desk. "Let me look at you." She told him to fix his hair but told Jordan she looked great.

Milo fixed his hair and even used his electric razor. The interviewers arrived with cameras and a few lights. They set up quickly, and their questions were about the same as those that had been asked a hundred times before. They wanted to know how Milo and Jordan worked; what techniques they employed to solve complex crimes. Milo was tired of saying the same things over and over, but he knew that these syndication interviews would appear all over the country. As always, Jordan was gracious as she smiled and gave great answers. The crew snapped a few shots of them in the office and thanked them for their time.

Jordan told Milo after that; they needed to get away for the day. They both said goodbye to Carol who waved and asked, "How did you do? I heard a lot of the same answers." Milo said, "How many ways can you say the same things? We'll see you tomorrow."

Once in the car, Milo asked where she would like to go. Jordan patted him on the tummy. "We've been pigging out too much lately, so I think we're both doing salads for a week." Milo begrudgingly agreed as he headed for a restaurant that served all-you-can-eat salads.

CHAPTER 4

Forbes and Associates

10:45 AM the next day

Milo glanced at his watch. "We made good time getting here." He slowed the car as they looked for the address. Jordan couldn't believe the location. "You sure this is the right place? This is a residential neighborhood." Milo assured his partner that this was the place. "I saw a photo on their website." They rolled through the impressive gates and drove up the long driveway. Milo parked in front of the ivy-covered Beverly Hills mansion and checked the address again. "Yes, this is it." Jordan stepped onto the parking area and looked up at the stately, double story home. She noticed the small Forbes & Associates sign near the front door. "You're right; this *is* the place."

They entered the reception area, and a charming, well-dressed secretary welcomed them. Milo presented his business card. "Thank you, Mr. Starr, I'm Della." Milo introduced his partner. "Can I get either of you something to drink?" Milo and Jordan said they were fine, for now. Della used her wireless phone connection to announce them and then escorted the P.I. duo to the main office. James Forbes greeted his guests and asked Della to notify his wife about the meeting. "And, please make sure we're not disturbed." She nodded, handed Mr. Forbes the business card and closed the door. James Forbes thanked them for coming so quickly. "Please have a seat. I'm sure the interviews and other publicity surrounding the cases you've solved must be keeping you super busy." Milo smiled, "Yes, it's been non-stop business since we hit the public spotlight, but we're not complaining."

Jordan was looking around the office. "We weren't sure this was the place since it doesn't look like a normal CPA firm." "You're right; it doesn't. This was my father's office, and when he retired, we took over." Milo noticed the curio cases against the wall and was going to ask about them when Kate Forbes entered. She, like her husband, was wearing upscale business attire.

Milo and Jordan stood as James introduced Kate, his wife, and partner. She thanked the Private Investigators for coming so quickly and invited them to sit on the couch and relax. She touched her ear and said, "Della, please bring us some coffee. Thank you." Kate asked about their current workload. Jordan explained that they had a lot of new client calls and had been on stakeouts for many nights in a row. Kate wondered if they had any free time currently. Jordan smiled and after looking at Milo said, "It really depends on the requirements of the case."

James placed a file marked '**The Golden Oasis Hotel**' on the coffee table. He also handed each of them a very expensive-looking promotional brochure and explained, "This is one of our businesses. My father owned this Las Vegas hotel, and now it's ours." Jordan began to look over the beautiful brochure. "This is lovely. I've heard of the hotel, but I've never been there." Kate smiled, "It really is a first-class, five-star property. We love the place but we're having trouble there, and that's why we called you." James added, "We've read about you solving some big crimes here in L.A. and then we saw one of your TV interviews. That's when we wondered if you could help us."

Della entered with a coffee service and asked if they needed anything else. James said, "No, we're okay for now. Thank you." When she closed the office door, James continued, "Let me explain what's going on at the hotel. Some of our guests have found erroneous charges on their credit card statements. We don't know how many are involved or how long it's been going on."

Kate handed Jordan a cup of coffee and said, "We work here and fly to Las Vegas to visit the hotel several times a month, but we can't keep track of everything." James told them they employ a lot of managers for the hotel, the casino, food and beverage and then a general manager who oversees everything." Milo took a sip of his coffee. "This is delicious, what's the brand?" Kate smiled, "It's mine. I roast and blend the coffee every week." James smiled as he said, "And she won't tell anyone her secret. Just like you won't tell anyone how you solved the mutilation murders." Milo smiled, "Well, it's very good coffee, and you should never give away the secret. How do you think we can help you, Mr. Forbes?"

James looked at Kate who nodded for him to proceed. "Well, first I'm James, and she's Kate, and we wondered if you could visit our hotel and stay for a week or so, all expenses paid, of course." Kate jumped in. "We want you to shop, eat, visit the spa, gamble, go to the shows, just enjoy everything the hotel has to offer and charge it all on a special credit card." Jordan loved the idea because they needed a vacation, but asked, "What's the catch?"

Kate told them all they had to do was keep track of everything they spend and what they buy. "Then we'll compare your notes with the credit card statements." James reminded them, "We only learned about this recently, and we need to know how deep it goes and who's doing it." Jordan asked, "What kind of charges did you find?" James opened the hotel file and handed Milo a copy of a credit card statement. "Note the charges we highlighted. They aren't real."

James passed the statement to Jordan who looked at the figures. "These are small, one is for thirty-two dollars, and this one is for twelve. You're sure they weren't legitimate charges?" Kate assured them that they talked with the cardholder who was positive the charges were fraudulent. "Notice that the charges are for bar drinks. The owner of the card is allergic to alcohol. That's how all this started." James told them that several other guests had reported similar findings. "We've reimbursed all the claims so far, but we have to find out who's doing it and stop it."

Kate said, "We noticed that charges were almost all the same amounts. That's when we realized we had trouble." James looked at Milo and Jordan. "I know it's not the kind of case you usually handle, but we remembered that the FBI liaison said you thought way outside the box. I think that's what we need here." Jordan looked at Milo and smiled. "We've been working non-stop since the FBI press conference and the subsequent interviews, so getting away would be like a dream." Milo smiled, "Our firm is called Sutton and Starr. That means whatever Ms. Sutton wants, she gets." James laughed and jokingly said, "That's the way it is around here too." Kate smacked him on the arm and said. "He's kidding you know." Milo added, "So was I."

James was very happy. "When do you think you could leave?" Jordan explained that they had several cases to wrap up. "Give us a few days to get everything taken care of. We could be ready by the end of next week." They all shook hands, and James asked if they would join him and his wife for lunch. "We can outline the plan a little further." Milo said yes, and Kate called Della to say that there would be two more for lunch. "We have a great kitchen and our employees eat here every day." Milo and Jordan accepted the invite because they liked these people and the setting and lunch smelled great.

During their continuation meeting over onion soup and a Cobb salad, they decided to fly to Las Vegas at the end of the following week. "That will give us a few days to take care of several on-going cases." James told them that they should act like newlywed tourists. Kate wondered if staying together in the same room was a problem.

Milo laughed, "Not a problem for us. We've lived together for quite a while now." James smiled, "You need to keep a low-profile, but I do want you to meet Carl, our internet guy who's been trying to find out who's behind all of this, but he hasn't had any success." Milo wanted to know how they found out about the charges. "Carl brought this mess to our attention. He was forwarded an email from a visitor who was inquiring about their extra charges." Jordan wondered why he received the email. "It was misdirected to him, since our General Manager, Sam Boyle is out for a medical procedure." James told them that Carl handled the reverse of funds and then he received a second notice about extra charges. "That's when Carl decided to investigate the files to see if this had happened before. When he found reversed charges approved by the G.M. going back over a year, he called me." Jordan asked, "You know Carl isn't involved with this, right?" James laughed, and Kate said, "No, it's not Carl. He's been with the hotel for over ten years." James added, "Since we don't know who's involved, he's the only employee we want you to meet. We'll keep everybody else in the dark for now."

Milo asked, "How long has your General Manager been with you?" James thought for a moment and looked at Kate. "When did Ralph Watkins retire?" Kate wasn't sure. "It was two years ago, I think." James explained that Ralph was the GM of the hotel when his father owned it and is now living in Florida with his family. "Would you like to speak with Ralph?" Milo said, "Maybe later, but let's see what's going on first."

Their lunch was fantastic. It was on par with the fanciest places in Beverly Hills.

James and Kate escorted Sutton and Starr to their car. James and Kate thanked them for coming and saying yes to their proposal. Milo smiled, "You made us an offer we can't refuse." Kate laughed and told them to send an email with their address, so their driver could pick them up for the flight. "Will do. See you next Thursday."

Milo was all smiles as they turned toward their condo. "So? What do you think?" Jordan was also grinning as she kicked off her new shoes and settled back in the super-soft seat. "Well, first, thank you for insisting that we dress up for this meeting. Next, I'm glad you had the car washed and waxed and this sounds like the dream job that we can't mention to Carol." Milo suddenly realized that she was right. "That's true! We'll just say we're going on a stakeout. She doesn't have to know that it's in Las Vegas."

Jordan closed her eyes and whispered. "Just make sure if we talk to her, we don't do it in the casino." She was quiet for a few moments and then opened her eyes again. "We also can't tell her about their office. If she hears they serve lunch to their employees, we're really screwed!" They both laughed at that notion.

"Almost forgot, you owe me dinner tonight." Milo kept driving without talking. "Did you hear me?" Milo glanced in her direction. "I know. I'm just thinking about where. Do you have a preference? Burgers, steak, hot dogs, what?" Jordan thought for a moment. "Okay, how about candlelight and wine, overlooking Waikiki beach." Milo laughed at that idea. "That's not gonna happen, but I'll think of something."

Back in the office, Carol was shocked to see them dressed up. "Where did you go today? Jordan started toward her office. "We met with a new client. Tell you about it later." She slipped into her office and called Mrs. Davis to set up a meeting then went over her call-back list. She made two appointments for early the following week. Milo also spent the day making calls to set up a few appointments. He knew they couldn't take any meetings the week after, as they would be in Las Vegas. He broke the news to Carol that they would be away on a stakeout starting next Thursday for about seven to ten days. "You get seven to ten days off with pay." Carol loved that idea. "I'll forward the calls to my cell and home phone and sleep late."

He asked Jordan to join him in his office. "How would you feel about giving Carol part of the money we got from the FBI?" Jordan hugged him. "I love the idea. How much?"

Milo opened their checkbook. "I don't know." Jordan held up five fingers. Milo never missed a chance to fool around. "Five dollars? That will work." She glared at him. "Okay, Five hundred." She shook her head no. "Okay, I'll add another zero." Jordan smiled because that was perfect. He wrote the check. "You give it to her." Jordan smiled again as she entered the foyer. "Carol, we have a surprise for you."

Their super-efficient office manager looked up and wondered what was going on. "The other day Milo and I received something from the FBI and you wanted to know what was in the envelope." Carol eagerly awaited the answer. "It was a check for services rendered and we would like to share it with you." She handed the gift to Carol who looked at it and couldn't believe the amount. "You're giving me five-grand?" Milo stood at his office doorway and smiled as Jordan said, "You deserve it." She pointed to Milo, "You've had to put up with him." Carol laughed and thanked them for the check. "This will come in handy. Thank you." Milo said, "We're out of here. See you tomorrow." Carol hugged them both as she said, "Get going, I'll close up."

CHAPTER 5

Evening on the Town

Sutton and Starr drove away from the office feeling a lot better than when they arrived. Milo was smiling and asked if Jordan wanted to go out for steaks. She said, "Sounds great as long as they have dessert." Milo asked, "Did you see the flyer we received about the new steakhouse down the street from the condo?" Jordan didn't know anything about a new restaurant, but was all for giving it a try. They parked in their garage and made a quick stop at the condo to freshen-up for dinner. Jordan was ready quickly because she was very hungry.

It was a strange feeling just walking arm-in-arm down their street to a fancy restaurant. When they approached the new 'in-spot,' the name really made them laugh. They entered and the young hostess at the reception desk greeted them. "Good evening, welcome to Jordan's Steakhouse." They looked over the interior and were very impressed. It was beautiful. The glow of the candles on each table and the colorful effect lighting on the walls made for a very elegant and inviting setting.

They were escorted to a perfect table on an up-raised area toward the rear of the room. From that location, they could survey the entire place. Jordan was smiling. Their attentive waiter asked if they would like to try the house wine. Jordan told him to pour. "This is a wonderful addition to our neighborhood." Milo agreed and began to look over the extensive menu, as a well-dressed gentleman approached their table. "Good evening, welcome to my restaurant, I'm William Jordan." Milo introduced himself and the restaurant's namesake, Jordan Sutton. Mr. Jordan smiled and asked, "Do you live in the area?" Jordan told him that it was only a short walk from their condo. The owner hoped they would like the place well enough to return. "If you give me your email address, I'll make sure you get some special offers." Milo handed him a business card. "We're both at that email address."

Mr. Jordan mentioned, "Business is still slow, but we've only been open a couple of weeks. I'm sure word-of-mouth will eventually bring in the customers. Please let your friends know that we're here." The owner left them with a smile and thanked them again for coming in. Jordan smiled and looked across the table. "Okay, no more work tonight." Milo was about to agree when he received a text. He looked at the phone. "It's an offer to download something I think we can use. It's an electronic device scanner." Jordan asked, "Don't we already have scanners?" Milo clicked the download button, "Yes, but this says it will make my phone into a portable scanner. It's included free with our scanner account. I'll give it a try."

They had a terrific evening. The professional piano player and international cuisine were first-class. The well-stocked bar was a big hit with Milo. "I think it's great to be able to drink and not have to worry about driving home." Jordan smiled and touched his drinking hand. "Guess what? We only made it one day on our new salad diet." Milo nodded, "And I went almost a full day without drinking. Cheers." He asked when they were going to the gym again. Jordan looked at her cell phone calendar. "I'm going later this week. Do you wanna join me?"

Milo folded his napkin. "I'll join you for some exercise and we'll re-start that diet thing again tomorrow." He looked at Jordan without saying a word. She felt a little embarrassed and had to ask, "What?" Milo smiled and took her hand. "I just wanted you to know that I love being with you." She smiled and squeezed his hand as he settled the tab. "And I enjoy being with you too. I'll show you how much, when we get home."

The owner caught them at the door. "I hope you enjoyed your evening with us." Milo said it was very nice. Jordan added that she liked having a first-class restaurant named after her. "We'll be back." The staff thanked them and off they went, arm in arm. Jordan put her head on his shoulder as they walked. "We better go to bed early-ish tonight because we have a busy day tomorrow. We're meeting with Mrs. Davis." Milo gave her a quick rundown of his schedule which included finishing up his extensive call list. "It's amazing how many new clients we have from the publicity on that one case."

Milo hit the shower first and was relaxing under the gentle spray. He started smiling and was slightly startled when Jordan joined him under the semi-warm water. "Oh, I didn't know this was a doubles shower." She opened the bath gel and began to apply it on his wet skin. He was super aroused to have Jordan soaping him up everywhere. They kissed, and he caressed her warm slippery body pulling her close. Jordan leaned against the shower wall and coaxed him by saying, "Come on big boy show me what you can do." Milo didn't have to be asked twice. He performed brilliantly under the cascading water and when he left the shower, he was clean, wet and totally drained; so much so, that he hoped he could get out of bed in the morning.

CHAPTER 6

Business as Usual

Milo kept smiling at Jordan and she made cute faces at him too. Carol watched their mating ritual as she arranged the beautiful flowers the two lovebirds brought in. She decided not to get involved. Milo was trying to wake up by gulping his morning coffee. He started making notes on his desk calendar about their impending week-long stakeout when Jordan asked, "You do plan to meet Mrs. Davis with me today, right?" He stopped writing. "Of course, since I did the stakeout on her husband, I'm sure I can add a few things." He straightened up his desk while Jordan placed one of her fragrant candles on his coffee table. She also brought in all the cosmetics she purchased from Mr. Davis and arranged them attractively on Milo's desk.

Carol made a pot of coffee and some hot water for tea. They were ready for Mrs. Davis who was on time and joined them in Milo's office. "Would you like coffee or tea?" She smiled, "Tea would be delightful." Mrs. Davis, who was wearing another tasteful outfit, wasted no time. She asked if they had watched her husband. "Yes, Milo followed him." She looked across his desk. "So, Mr. Starr, what did you learn?"

Milo looked at the lovely lady and hoped what he was about to tell her would make her happy. "Mrs. Davis, from what I saw during my stakeout and found on-line, I have concluded that your husband is not having an affair." She looked shocked. "What? Then why does he smell like other women?" Jordan pointed toward the jars and boxes on the desk. "Do you use these products?" Mrs. Davis looked at the array of cosmetic containers. "No, I don't." Jordan took a long pause and said, "I bought all these products from your husband."

"You bought them from Bradley?" Mrs. Davis gave Jordan a blank stare. "I don't understand." Milo saw that she seemed totally confused. "Let me explain everything." He told her about his stakeout and what he learned by following her husband. "I watched Mr. Davis an entire day. He had an insurance sales meeting out of the office then dropped by Beautee Cosmetics. I then followed him to a home in a nice residential area where he hosted a product party for six ladies before returning to the insurance company."

Jordon added, "After Milo's stakeout, I set up an appointment with your husband to show me the cosmetic line." Milo poured himself a cup of coffee. "He met with Jordan and our secretary Carol. They bought a lot of products." Jordan handed the husband's business card to Mrs. Davis. "He's known as Mr. Baker and he's the top salesperson at Beautee Cosmetics." Milo brought up the Beautee Cosmetics website and turned the screen toward their shocked client. "Here's his photo on their website."

Mrs. Davis looked at the screen and Jordan saw the tears in her eyes. "He doesn't have a girlfriend?" Jordan said, "No. He was very professional when he came here. He's a very good salesman, who really knows the product line." Mrs. Davis sat back in her chair and took a sip of her tea. "I'm totally embarrassed. I really thought he was having an affair. What should I do?"

Jordan told her what she thought would be the best battle plan. "Here's what I'd do. Just let things go along as they are for now." Milo added, "Your husband has a speaking engagement coming up for Beautee Cosmetics. Since he's their top sales person, I'm sure he'll mention the speech to you." Mrs. Davis asked why they thought he was doing this?

Milo asked about their finances. "Do you need money for anything special?" She paused for a moment, "Yes, for property taxes and college for our daughter." Jordan thought that might be the reason. The distraught wife looked at both of them, "Then why not tell me?" Jordan leaned in and quietly said, "Maybe he's embarrassed to be selling cosmetics." The wife said, "That might be it." She stood and thanked them for finding the answer.

"What do I owe you?" Jordan said they would send her an invoice. She escorted the smiling Mrs. Davis to the front door. "Remember, when he finally tells you about his second job, you should act surprised." Mrs. Davis said she would and thanked Jordan several times as she left. Jordan closed the door and Carol handed her a tissue. "Some of these cases really get me." Carol smiled and understood. "This feeling of actually helping someone is why I decided to join you guys."

Carol buzzed Milo. "*You have a call from James Forbes.*" "Hi James, this is Milo." James wanted to make sure that next Thursday was still good with them. "Yes, I have it written in ink. We're good to go. When will we know exactly what you want us to do?" James told him that Kate has been working on all of that. "We'll lay everything out for you on the plane. We need your address, so our driver can pick you up. Is nine AM okay?" Milo gave him their address and told him that they would be ready to go on time. "Thank you for deciding to help us. See you Thursday." Milo wrote 9 AM on his desk calendar.

Jordan popped in to say she finished her call list. "We have two new client meetings set for Monday. Carol has their info. Shall we get out of here?" Milo turned off his desk lamp and made a bee-line for the door. "Well? What are you waiting for?" Jordan laughed and said she'd be back in a moment. "I need to get my purse." Milo joined Carol. "We're leaving for the day, so you get out of here too." Carol smiled, "Great, I'll see you tomorrow?" Milo looked at her and said, "Tomorrow? No, we're not here tomorrow or Sunday and neither are you. See you Monday."

Milo started the car and Jordan asked where they were going. "We're going shopping. We both need a few outfits for our Las Vegas trip. I talked with James and they are picking us up at nine on Thursday morning." Jordan loved the idea of going shopping. "I do need some new shoes. What are we doing tomorrow?" Milo smiled. "That's easy, I'm sleeping all day. Same schedule Sunday."

CHAPTER 7

New Case Day

When Milo and Jordan arrived at the office, Carol couldn't believe how good Milo looked. He didn't have any beard stubble, he had a haircut and she thought he might be wearing some new clothes. "Is that a new shirt?" Milo grunted and nodded as he entered his office. Carol followed him, "What's the occasion?" Jordan answered, "We went shopping." Carol couldn't believe it. "Mr. Starr went shopping and actually bought something?" Jordan told her, "It was like pulling teeth, but he got some new duds." Carol headed back to her desk smiling. "Your first appointment will be along soon."

Jordan straightened up the coffee table and Milo cleared his desk. He took a moment to check his email. "Look at this. There are six new client inquiries all from our website." Milo buzzed Carol. *"Please access the mail and print out the new client inquiry forms."* Jordan couldn't believe everything that was happening. "Do you know how many clients we've gotten because of the interviews and print stories?" Milo didn't know for sure. "Let's ask Carol." Milo started to buzz her and before he could touch the button, she buzzed him. *"Mr. Starr your first appointment is here."* Milo looked at Jordan and mouthed the words, "Mr. Starr." He grinned and told Carol he was ready.

Carol opened the door and an extremely very well-dressed, self-assured young lady entered quickly dismissing Carol with a flick of her calfskin gloves. She extended her hand to Jordan as she said, "Hello Jordan. I know you because I saw one of your television interviews, I'm Kristy Merrill. Thank you for taking time to meet with me." Jordan shook the young lady's hand and introduced her partner. Kristy extended her hand to Milo as if she was the Pope waiting for him to kiss the ring. Milo took her hand and loved her super soft skin. He lowered his voice and asked, "What can we do for you Ms. Merrill?"

She slowly took back her hand and looked approvingly around the office. The aloof client used her gloves to brush off the chair before she sat. Without saying a word, she turned on her phone. "I've been robbed. The bastards took my favorite painting." She showed Milo a photo of the missing artwork. He took the phone and turned it toward Jordan. "When did this happen?" She asked for the phone back and brought up her calendar. "It happened two weeks ago yesterday." Milo asked, "What size is the painting? It's difficult to tell from the photo."

She glared at Milo. "Size?" She looked around the office and pointed to a framed designer photo on the back wall. "It's about the size of your Twin Tower's lithograph." Milo made a note, "Okay, three by four feet. Who is the artist?" She quickly changed the subject. "That's not important. What *is* important is, I want to know that I've chosen the right agency to solve my problem."

Jordan jumped in to ask, "Ms. Merrill did you call the police?" Kristy looked at her and almost snarled as she said, "Yeah, but those assholes couldn't find a hooker in a whore house! That's why I'm here." Jordan shut up after that outburst. Milo asked if she would send them a copy of the photo. She picked up his business card from the desk and clicked a few buttons on her phone. "I just sent it to you." Milo smiled, "Thank you. We've located quite a few paintings, so I think we *can* help you." She stood and took a walk around the office checking out their very up-scale décor. "I know you've recovered a lot of things and solved some big headline cases. I've read up on both of you. So, where do we start?" Milo nodded to Jordan who said. "Well, we'll need to know where you kept the painting and how the thieves got in. Was it insured?"

The snarky new client turned to Jordan. "The painting was in my home. I have an alarm system with cameras, but they didn't trip the alarm and the video was blank." Milo said, "So, it sounds like a professional job. How much is the painting worth?" "That's not important. It was my favorite, *that's* what's important. People should have their favorite things near them all the time." She stopped "acting" for a moment and looked at them. "The jackasses at the insurance company said I must not have armed the alarm system, so they aren't helping very much. I always set the alarm. Always! Do you think you can help me?"

Milo told her they would like to see the location where the painting was hung and check out the alarm system. "Can we do that tomorrow?" Kristy thought that was a great idea. She slapped her hands with the gloves. "You people work fast, I like that." She put her card on Milo's desk. "Can you come at ten?" Jordan said that would be perfect. The young lady stood and thanked them. As she headed for the door she stopped. "I forgot one important thing. When they took the painting, they let my dog escape. I'll send you Tonto's photo and if you can find him too, I'd be very grateful and pay you double your fee." She slapped her gloves to her hand, nodded and left the office as quickly as she arrived.

Milo paused a few moments after the outside doors closed. He looked at Jordan and asked, "Well, what's your opinion of her?" Jordan sat on the couch. "I would call her a bitch, but that's not being fair to all the bitches of the world. I feel very sorry for her dog. I hope we can find him." Milo laughed, "Maybe the dog saw an open door and said, I want out of here." He wandered over to Carol's desk. "We finally got a lost dog case." She laughed and applauded. "It's about time." "We're going to Ms. Merrill's home in the morning to check out the scene of the crime." Carol made a note. "What's her address and phone number?" Jordan handed over the new client's business card. "Thank you, your second meeting is at two." Milo looked at the clock on the wall. "We have an hour, anybody hungry?" Jordan and Carol raised their hands at the same time. "Do you guys practice that?" They both laughed and asked where they were going? "Since we only have an hour, how about I get us something from the taco truck?"

Carol and Jordan groaned, "It's okay this time, especially if you're buying." Milo asked what they wanted. "Anything you pick." He turned and left the office and about two minutes later he was on the street. The taco truck was right on time. He got in line and thought about his order. He didn't have to wait long. "I'll have twelve small tacos to go, no onions." He thought that would take a long time, but he paid and a few minutes later the "official truck lady" said, "Twelve for Milo." He smiled and took his bag of tasty treasures to the office. When he arrived, Carol and Jordan were waiting on his couch in his office. They had the coffee table set up for food with three soft drinks, forks and napkins. "Great, let's eat." He opened the bag. Jordan did a fast count. "You bought a dozen?" Milo opened his first small street taco. "Sure, they aren't big and what we have left over Carol can take home."

They ate and talked about business. "Carol, have we had any new client calls?" She tried not talking with a mouth full of taco. "Yes, the publicity just keeps them coming. Today, you had three client calls and two interview calls from magazines. You're going to be famous again." They finished lunch without being interrupted by the phone and Carol put six tacos in the small fridge to take home. "Your next meeting is in fifteen minutes." Jordan and Milo straightened the office and Carol sprayed all around to get rid of the taco aroma. "I think we need some scented candles too!" Carol retrieved a large one from the lobby desk and put it on Milo's desk. "That's better."

Jordan and Milo made phone calls while they waited for their second meeting. Milo spoke quickly with James Forbes about their impending trip to Vegas. "Yes, we're ready to go, see you Thursday morning." He checked his email and found one from Kristy, their first appointment of the day, with two attachments. One was a shot of the painting and the other was a photo of Tonto, a cute little white poodle.

Milo looked up and saw his partner. "Jordan, I think I'll send the photo of Ms. Merrill's painting to our favorite pawnbroker, Baldy." Jordan thought that was a great idea. "Tell him there's a reward." Milo looked at his lady, "There's a reward?" Jordan laughed and said, "Sure, there's always a reward." "Right! Good idea." He drafted a fast email and attached the picture of the painting. "Let's see what happens; Baldy has come through for us many times." Carol stepped in to tell them that their next meeting had to be postponed.

"Remember we're out of town for at least seven to ten days. Starting next Thursday." "I know. I set the meeting for the end of the month." Jordan wanted to know what kind of case it was. Carol checked her notepad. "It's insurance fraud. Sounds pretty involved." Milo told her that setting it for the end of the month was a good call. "Remember the last fraud case we did? It took us over two months to wrap that one up." Jordan remembered and wondered if they were finished for the day.

Milo looked at Carol who said, "You're asking me?" Milo smiled at her, "Yes, I'm asking you. Are we done for the day?" Carol suddenly felt the power of her position. "Yes, we are finished today. I'll see you both tomorrow." Milo turned off his desk lamp. "Thank you, boss." He and Jordan started to leave when Carol reminded them to dress up a little tomorrow afternoon. "You have two interviews, one for a magazine and one for a newspaper." "I'll make sure he looks presentable." Carol nodded at Jordan. "Okay, let's go."

CHAPTER 8

A Fast Week

Milo and Jordan arrived at Kristy Merrill's decorator home at exactly ten AM. Her maid met them at the door, invited them into the foyer, and asked them to remove their shoes. They complied with the request and followed the well-dressed maid to the solarium where they were greeted by Ms. Merrill. "Thank you for coming, and for being prompt." She touched an empty space. "This is where my painting hung." She pointed to six small circles on the wall. "Notice these pressure switches behind the painting? If it's moved even an inch, the alarm would have triggered. The bastards even defeated those." Jordan asked if they could see the main alarm panel. The lady of the house led them to a small closet just off the kitchen. Milo looked at the panel and asked Jordan if she thought it had been compromised. "I don't see any indication of that." Milo glanced around the very expensive-looking kitchen and asked if anything other than the painting was missing. Kristy said she'd looked all over the house and everything seemed to be untouched. Jordan moved to the back door and lightly touched it as she attempted to inspect the lock. The door swung wide-open.

Jordan closed the back door and asked Kristy if she would arm her alarm system. Kristy touched her intercom and told her maid that she was going to set the alarm system as a test. She then moved to the panel and entered her code. The system beeped once, and the red-armed light switched on. "Okay, the system is armed." Jordan once again crossed to the back door and touched it. The door opened, and it did not alert the alarm system. Kristy was shocked. "What the hell is wrong? Is my alarm system broken? Milo told her to test the system by opening the window over the sink. When she opened that window just two inches the alarm panel began to beep. The female alarm voice said, "Disarm the system. You have thirty seconds." Kristy quickly entered her code and the alarm voice said, "Disarmed, ready to arm." She looked at Milo, "What the hell just happened?"

Jordan, looking at the contact on the rear door found the problem, "This door has been removed from your system. This is how they got in undetected. Have you had any alarm work done recently?" "No, I haven't." Milo said, "It might have been done a long time ago. Do you enter the house through this door?" She told them that she always enters from the garage. "I've never used this door to enter." Jordan asked if the police checked the alarm system. "No, they just looked at the panel and that's about it."

Milo advised her to contact her alarm company and have them do a complete system analysis. "Then change your password." She thanked them for finding the problem and said she hoped it would be that easy for them to find her painting and her little dog. Jordan suddenly felt very sympathetic for the young lady. Even if she wasn't the most likable client, Jordan could tell that this intrusion, this violation into her personal space, was very upsetting. Jordan said, "We have the photo of your painting and the cute picture of Tonto, we'll get right to work to see what we can do for you."

Kristy smiled, thanked them for coming and said quietly, "Call me if you need any additional information. I'm glad you found the problem." Milo assured her that they would contact her, the instant they learned anything. As they drove to the office Milo looked over at Jordan and smiled. "You did great today Ms. Sutton. I can't believe the police didn't find that the back door wasn't in the system." She laughed, "Well to quote our client, they couldn't find a hooker in a house of ill-repute. I cleaned up the quote for your tender ears."

The afternoon went fast. Milo and Jordan floated through their interviews. They had done so many for newspapers, radio and TV over the past few months that they were pros at talking about what they do. The one question Milo still would not answer is, "How did you solve the city-wide mutilation murders"? Each time that's asked, Jordan knows it's her cue to jump in. "Sorry, but he won't tell you how we did it and neither will I." Milo always uses a line he's used in every interview. "We just used deductive reasoning." Following the interviews, they spent the next few days interviewing potential clients on the phone while at the office and packing at night.

"Carol, we'll be on our cell phones. You can forward the calls to your home, sleep-in as late as you want, and we'll be back here next week." Carol always loved her time away from the office. As her P.I.'s started to leave, she blocked their path. "You're not running off to get married, are you?" Jordan assured her that wasn't in their plans. "Good, because if that ever happens and I'm not invited, I'll hunt you down." Milo hugged his long-time friend. "Carol, you have nothing to worry about." As Milo and Jordan walked down the hall he said, "I was going to whistle the wedding march." Jordan punched him in the arm. "Glad you didn't because Carol would have been pissed."

THURSDAY 8:30 AM

Milo and his medium-size suitcase were waiting in the living room. Jordan asked if he could help with her bags. "Bags? What are you taking?" She didn't give him an answer. She just rolled her large case into the living room and put her carry-on bag next to it. They didn't have to wait very long because the limo was right on time. Milo answered the door and was greeted by a gentleman in a dark suit and tie. "Good morning Mr. Starr, I'm Marcus. Let me get those bags for you." Jordan grabbed her purse while Milo set the alarm, and locked up. Their driver helped them to the car, opened the rear door for them and put their bags in the trunk. "If you need anything, just ask. I filled the thermal mugs with coffee." Milo never said no to coffee. He settled into the soft seat and took a sip. He knew right away that this was Kate's special blend. The trip was off to a smashing start.

He smiled at Jordan and handed her a thermal mug. They both relaxed on the way to the airport.

Jordan leaned over to Milo and whispered quietly, "I think we're gonna love this job." Milo leaned towards her, "You've been to Las Vegas before." She sipped her coffee and whispered, "Sure, but never as a high-roller." Milo touched his mug to hers. They both were smiling as Marcus cruised along the freeway. "How's the air temperature for you?" Jordan told the driver it was perfect.

The ride to the private jet didn't take long. They pulled up to the entry gate and Marcus lowered his window and the rear passenger window. The guard looked at his credentials and then glanced at Milo and Jordan. Marcus raised the windows as the limo rolled slowly toward the far end of the airfield. The car stopped, and the driver opened the rear door for the guests. They stepped onto the tarmac and saw their clients, James and Kate, waiting in front of a sleek corporate jet. James greeted them and smiled, "Good morning, I hope you're ready for a fabulous time." Jordan noticed that Marcus was getting their bags. "Thank you, Marcus." He smiled and rolled their bags toward the plane. Milo saw the suitcases and laughed, "James, my bag is the small one." Kate said, "I always travel with a large case." James nodded, "Yes, she always takes everything she owns." Kate took Jordan's arm and escorted her up the small stairway. "Ladies have to look good all the time. Guys just don't get it." The girls laughed as they entered the plane.

During the flight, they were served a continental breakfast and were briefed for their Las Vegas escapade.

James gave each of them a packet of information. "Let me run through everything with you. You each have a Platinum Gaming Card. Use them when you play any table game or slot machine. Whatever you win is yours to keep. These are credit cards with a one-hundred-thousand-dollar line of credit for each of you. Charge everything and keep track of every dime you spend, what you bought and where you used it."

Milo thanked James and Kate for calling them to help solve this problem. Jordan said, "Looking over the list I see we're going to be busy." Kate told her, "I know there are lots of things to do inside the hotel, but you should be able to do everything." James agreed and added, "I don't want you to be too busy to play a few games of chance." Milo assured him that they would make time to play. "Jordan loves Keno and poker machines." Jordan grinned, "Yes I do." Kate reminded them to use their player cards everywhere. "Here's something you'll need." She handed Jordan a thick envelope. Inside was a two-inch stack of one-hundred-dollar bills. "This is for incidentals that require cash. Keno, the Sports Book and tips to porters and the housekeeping staff. Things like that."

Jordan thanked them and put the envelope in her purse. James checked the list on his phone. "I think that's it. Any questions?" Milo finished his coffee and asked about meeting their computer guy. "We'll text you about that. In fact, I'll text you during the week if we think of anything else we need you to do." Kate looked at their guests and smiled. "We have one more item for you." She reached in her purse and handed each of them a small dark purple velvet bag. James said, "I almost forgot about that!"

Milo opened his little bag, looked inside and paused. He waited for Jordan to open hers. When she looked, she smiled, and didn't know what to say. Kate asked, "What do you think?" Jordan withdrew a very expensive-looking wedding ring from her bag. "We figured you couldn't act like a young married couple without rings." Milo removed his plain gold band and tried it on. "Wow it fits." Jordan was hesitant, but seeing that Milo was wearing his, she slipped on her ring and held up her hand for all to see. "It's beautiful." Kate nodded, "Yes they are, but you have to give them back when you wrap up your investigation. They are on loan from a jewelry store in Beverly Hills."

Jordan and Milo said they would guard the rings and thanked James and Kate for thinking of everything. Jordan sat back, looked at the ring and laughed. James wondered what the joke was. "When we left the office, our wonderful secretary asked if we were running away to get married." Milo added, "We told her that wasn't going to happen. So, if she ever sees these rings, we'd be in deep trouble." Everyone laughed as their pilot announced their approach to the Las Vegas airport.

They buckled up and prepared to land. Jordan was very excited about their upcoming week away from the office. She was also smiling as she looked at her beautiful ring. The landing was smooth and the temperature in the desert was perfect. James shook hands with their guests. "Milo, you and Jordan take the limo, we'll take our car. When you check in at the hotel, please notice the cameras above the main desk.

Just look up at the camera for a moment. Carl, our computer guy, will grab a frame of your faces and then follow you during your entire trip." Milo understood and assured them that they would do that for sure. Kate hugged them both and said, "James and I want to thank you again for helping us." Milo and Jordan entered the limo and headed for The Golden Oasis Hotel.

They gawked at the opulence of the Vegas Strip just like every tourist does and felt as if they were on cloud nine when they pulled up to the very exclusive hotel. Their driver opened the rear door, helped them out of the limo and handed them his card. "If you need to go anywhere during your trip, Mr. and Mrs. Forbes said to call me." They thanked the driver as a bellman joined them. "Checking in?" They indicated yes as the driver and bellman loaded their bags onto the transfer cart. The porter escorted them to the front desk.

Milo handed their paperwork to the receptionist and while she checked on their reservation they both looked up at the security camera. A moment later she found their reservation and handed their bellman a small folder. "Please show Mr. and Mrs. Starr to Suite A." The bellman nodded and stood to one side. Jordan reached into her purse and handed the young lady at the desk a hundred-dollar bill from her stash. "Can you change this for me?" The lady nodded and said, "Yes, are twenty's and ten's okay?" Jordan said that would be fine. Money in-hand they turned to follow the bellman to their suite.

They entered the express elevator and the well-dressed bellman pushed 22. He smiled at Milo and Jordan and asked if they were on their honeymoon.

Jordan realized that they had to start playing the game. "Yes, we are. Does it show?" He smiled and said, "Yes, it's hard to miss." They stepped out on the 22nd floor and noticed that their suite was directly opposite the elevator. The bellman told them that there were only four suites on this floor. "It's very exclusive; you won't have any visitors." He opened the wide blade shutters to display the splendor of the Vegas Strip and asked if they needed anything else. Jordan handed him twenty dollars. "Not right now, thank you." He indicated that their bags were already in the closet as he closed the door.

When they were alone, Milo opened his cell phone and began to move around the mini-suite. "What are you doing, taking photos of the room?" Milo showed her the screen. "I'm using my new app to scan for electronic listening devices. You know I always check hotel rooms." Jordan understood. He finished his scan. "All clear." She tested the bed and reminded him to start taking notes on what they spend. Milo made a note on his cell phone. "Tips. How much?" Jordan headed to the bathroom. "Twenty dollars." Milo made the notation. "I'm hungry, where do you want to eat and when?" She said, "How about the buffet?" Milo agreed. "Early lunch at the buffet and then late dinner somewhere else." He put his player card and special credit card in his money clip and told Jordan to be sure to take hers as well. She handed him five-hundred in cash and put the balance of their cash in the hotel safe. She hoped they hadn't forgotten anything. "Let's get dressed for lunch." That sounded like a plan.

The Oasis Buffet was fantastic. The wait staff was very attentive, and the food was so well-prepared and displayed that it didn't seem like they were at a buffet. Milo wasn't talking; he was having too much fun eating. "Do you think we can dine here again during our trip?" Jordan thought it was possible, "But we have a lot of restaurants to cover this week."

As Milo headed for the dessert bar he said, "Well, I hope we can. Did you notice they make their own ice cream every day?" Jordan finished her coffee and told him, "If you eat like this the entire time we're here, you'll weigh three-hundred pounds by the time we get home." He shook his head, covered his ears and made a bee-line for the ice cream station.

The evening was nice. They walked around the hotel, played some Keno and had a few drinks. Jordan reminded her partner to be sure to keep track of what they were spending. He showed her the receipt from the buffet and their evening drinks. "I'm keeping track of everything." They turned in early. Jordan watched TV as Milo looked down at the ring on his finger and smiled. "We act just like an *old* married couple. We better change that tomorrow. We're supposed to be newlyweds." He looked over at Jordan who was nodding off with the TV remote in her hand. Milo quietly charged his phone, kissed Jordan lightly on the forehead and turned down the lights. He made a tall 7 & 7 and sat looking at the love of his life and the exciting lights of Las Vegas. He was too tired to do anything but sit, look and drink.

CHAPTER 9

Las Vegas - Day 4

Sutton and Starr were busy visiting many of the shops and restaurants on Kate's list and giving award-winning performances as newlyweds. Milo was keeping very accurate records of everything they did and spent. So far, neither of them noticed anything out of the ordinary. "What are we doing today?" Jordan checked her list and decided they would be visiting the salon. "We're each having a mani-pedi." Milo grunted as he asked, "Do we have to?" Jordan waved her palm in his face and said, "We've been here three days, it's time. We'll go right after breakfast."

Milo reluctantly accompanied Jordan to the spa. He loved the pedicure, but didn't want to admit it. Jordan, however, saw how pleased he looked when the very curvy attendant was massaging his feet. She smiled and wondered if he enjoyed this enough to do it when they got back to Los Angeles. Jordan had trouble holding in a laugh when his young lady asked if he wanted his nails polished. Milo stammered, "No, no, that's not necessary." He and Jordan paid using the special credit card, and she tipped both girls from her stash of cash. They left arm-in-arm and headed for the gigantic casino floor.

Milo guided them into The Dublin Pub, a bar just off the lobby that they hadn't visited yet. "We need a drink after that pedi-thing." Jordan laughed, "You know you loved it." As soon as they entered, Jordan knew this was Milo's kind of place. It was dark and quaint. The small table lamps on the bar added to the atmosphere and the bar stools were very plush and comfortable. Milo opened his cell phone and put it on the bar. He asked Jordan how much they spent so far that day. She rummaged in her slouch bag for a moment and handed him three receipts. "We haven't done much today." He began to list their expenditures as the tall, handsome bartender placed napkins in front of them. "Hello, I'm Tim. Welcome to The Dublin Pub, what can I get fur ya dear?" Jordan loved his slight Irish accent and smiled as she ordered a gin and tonic for each of them. "With a wee bit of lime?" Jordan nodded and said, "Yes, please."

As their drinks arrived one of their receipts floated to the floor. Milo bent down to retrieve it and noticed the electronic scanner on his phone was flashing. The bartender asked, "Will ya be needin' anything else?" Milo looked up as Jordan said, "No, thank you." Then he noticed that the flashing had stopped. He finished entering their expenditures on his phone and uploaded the information to their cloud server. He put the receipts in his wallet then raised his glass. "To you my dear. I hope you're enjoying our honeymoon."

Jordan stopped and then realized Milo was playing the married game. She smiled and kissed him on the cheek as she whispered, "Yes, and tonight I'll show you how much." Milo laughed and took a large swallow of his drink. The attentive barkeep asked, "Would ya' like another, sir?" Milo nodded yes and turned his attention to his lovely partner. He was about to tell her about the scanner when their drinks arrived, and the small red light flashed again.

Tim moved away, and the flashing stopped. Milo asked, "Tim, do you have any peanuts?" The Irish barkeep nodded and brought them a small bowl of munchies. As he approached, the light flashed again. This time Jordan saw the flash and was about to mention it to Milo who put his hand over the screen and shook his head no. Milo thanked Tim and took a few nuts from the bowl. He finished his drink and the bartender asked if they wanted another. Milo said no and put his special credit card on the bar. When Tim picked up the credit card, the light flashed again. Milo signed the tab and he and Jordan stepped out into the casino. "We need to talk, let's go up to our room."

Once in their suite Milo removed his phone, opened the scanner app, and checked the room again. It was clear. "I think I've found something, but I don't know what it is." He explained about the scanner app flashing each time the bartender in The Dublin Pub approached. "What does that mean?" Milo shook his head, "I don't know." She wondered if there was information online. Milo logged into his scanner account and found the answer to her question. "This app is connected to our full-service scanning account. It works just like the big scanners we use. This one comes alive and blinks when it senses an illegal listening device, credit card scanner, also known as a skimmer or any unauthorized camera. So, I think we found a credit card skimmer device. That Irish bartender must have been wearing it." Jordan told him to get dressed while she made a note to re-check the pub. "We may have found the problem. Why didn't we see it before?" Milo was changing his shirt and checked his hair. "Because I didn't have the app activated on my phone, or I just didn't notice. I'm getting hungry, let's go eat."

Jordan entered the huge bathroom to check her makeup. She asked, "Where do you want to go?" Milo didn't know for sure. He was looking out on the Vegas strip as the sun disappeared behind the luxurious hotels. "How about Mexican?" Jordan told him that there was a five-star Mexican restaurant in the hotel. "Call for reservations while I get dressed." Milo picked up the phone and didn't have to dial. The concierge desk answered immediately and made the reservation for them. "Call anytime, we're here to help you, Mr. Starr." Milo thanked the young lady and told Jordan they were eating at seven. "Let's have a drink before dinner." She emerged from the bathroom looking re-energized. "Where? At the pub?" Milo picked up his cell phone and nodded yes.

They entered The Dublin Pub and the attractive young Irish lass behind the bar smiled and said, "Good-evenin'. Welcome to The Pub, I'm Sally". Milo and Jordan pulled up comfortable bar stools as Sally placed napkins in front of them. "What'll ya have darlin'?" Jordan, who loved the extra attention said, "Some white wine please." Milo ordered a 7 & 7 for himself. He placed his cell phone on the bar and opened the scanner app. Jordan loved the subdued lighting. The glow from the small lamps along the bar set a cozy mood. She looked at the cell phone as Sally approached with their drinks. The app didn't flash but they were both shocked when the phone rang.

Milo saw the caller I.D. "Hi Carol. What's up?" He moved away from the bar to speak in private. Carol told him that Baldy called, "Something about a painting. Should I tell him to call you direct?" Milo said that would be fine. She wanted to know how the stakeout was going. "You're not in any danger, are you?" Milo looked around at his fancy surroundings and assured her they were fine. "I'm just checking. Call me tomorrow." Milo promised and joined Jordan at the bar. She asked, "Who called?" "It was our mother hen Carol checking up on us. She said that Baldy called about the painting. I told her to have him call us on our cells." Jordan raised her wine glass, "See? We're good. We solve crimes even when we're out of town, in a bar." The lovely bartender asked if they wanted another drink. Milo said, "Not right now, we have dinner reservations. We should leave." He put his special credit card on the bar and helped Jordan down from the bar stool. They signed the check and he handed Jordan the receipt. They stepped into the casino and headed for dinner.

On the way to the restaurant, Jordan played her favorite four Keno numbers for ten games. She said she'd check the numbers after they ate. Milo held his favorite lady around the waist as they crossed the casino floor. The place was very busy tonight with lots of gamblers playing slots, table games and drinking. They entered El Oro Mexicana and the hostess in a colorful, flowing dress checked their reservation.

"You're a little early Mr. Starr. Please give these coasters to the bartender. Enjoy complimentary Margaritas while you wait for your table to be prepared." Milo and Jordan took seats at the very large bar and handed the coasters to the bartender. He asked, "With or without salt?" They both said, "With salt, please." Jordan looked around the restaurant and loved the authentic decorations. "If the food is as good as the décor, we've got another winner." Their drinks arrived, and they toasted with the frosty glasses.

The couple next to them asked for their check and when the bartender crossed to the couple, Milo's phone buzzed in his pocket. He realized that he left the scanner app open. He waited for a moment and placed his phone on the bar. Jordan smiled at the couple next to them. "Nice place, huh?" The older lady said it was one of their favorites. The bartender handed the couple their credit card and Milo's cell began to flash again. He showed Jordan the phone. She raised her glass to him and whispered, "Looks like we're on a roll." Milo said, "Yes, I think we are." Milo's phone rang, and the caller ID said, "Baldy." He moved away from the bar and answered the call. "Hi Baldy, what's up?" Milo listened and smiled at Jordan. "You have the painting?" Baldy said he gave the guy $200 and the guy left it. Milo told him, "There's a reward, but I don't know how much." Baldly said, "Make it twelve-hundred and we'll call it even." Milo told him they would talk tomorrow.

A waitress wearing a beautiful, ruffled Mexican costume approached Jordan and Milo, "Mrs. Starr, your table is ready. We'll get your drinks for you." They thanked the bartender as a waiter put their drinks on a tray and followed them to their table. Jordan smiled and flashed her ring to Milo, "She called me Mrs. Starr." Milo leaned over and kissed her on the cheek, "Well, that means we must look the part." They had a very relaxing dinner. The service was outstanding as was the food. "Be sure to check this place off Kate's list." Jordan said she already did. Milo finished his second drink. "This is the best Margarita, and the best Mexican food on the planet!" Jordan laughed, "And you would know because you've eaten in every Mexican restaurant in the known world?" Milo shrugged his shoulders, "No, but it's the best Mexican food in this hotel." She agreed, it was fantastic then she patted his tummy. "No dessert for you."

Their waiter presented them with the check. Milo looked at the total and put his special credit card in the leather folder and placed his cell phone on the table as they waited for a waiter to pick up the card. The waiter collected the check and the cell phone flashed. Milo waited for a moment and looked at Jordan. "It's happening all over this place." Jordan finished her drink and leaned over to kiss her partner on the cheek. "Let's go. I want to check my Keno numbers and then head upstairs, if you're ready." Milo smiled and kissed his "wife de-jour" on the cheek. "I'm ready for a fantastic evening Mrs. Starr." She smiled, "I didn't forget about the marriage thing. I bought something today I want you to see."

They left the restaurant and stopped by the Keno lounge. Jordan checked her games and found out she was a winner. "Wow, I won a hundred and sixty dollars." She played another ten games and grabbed Milo's arm. "Let's go. I'm a big winner and you're in for a wonderful night." They took the express elevator to suite A and she raced into the room grabbing a pink boutique bag from the entry table as she headed to the bathroom. Milo entered, locked the door and opened the blackout drapes. While he waited for his "wife" he uncorked a bottle of chilled White Zinfandel and poured two glasses. He sat looking at the lights and the extremely bright LED signs on the Las Vegas strip.

Jordan emerged from the bathroom wearing a very alluring outfit. She whispered, "Hi stranger, are you looking for a good time tonight?" Milo turned away from the windows and was very surprised. This was the first time he ever saw Jordan wearing a frilly negligee. She usually slept in the nude. The love of his life looked like a runway model and suddenly Milo was very excited about what the evening might hold for him. His partner strutted her stuff around the room and asked if he liked her purchase? "Yes, I love it." She lowered herself onto Milo's lap and kissed him gently on the cheek. She smiled and whispered, "I thought you might." He moved her face a few inches and kissed her as if they were really married. She responded pressing her ample chest to his and moving around on his lap. "I think someone is ready for a honeymoon surprise."

Milo helped her up and closed the blackout drapes as she guided them to the king-size bed. Jordan smiled seductively and beckoned for her "husband" to join her.

A very eager Milo collapsed next to his loving partner. "Are you ready to play honeymoon night with me?" Jordan sat up and slowly removed her new lingerie, she smiled and said, "I'm ready, but I'm not sure about you, since you're a year older than me. That's kinda old you know!"

CHAPTER 10

Is it Morning?

Milo heard a cricket, or that's what he thought was making that sound. He opened his eyes a crack and realized it was his phone. "Hi, this is Milo." He continued to listen under his pillow. *"Milo, good morning, this is James Forbes. Kate and I wondered if you'd learned anything about our situation."* Milo sat up and moved away from his sleeping beauty. "Yes, I was going to call you today because we think we've discovered something."

James told him they arrived late last night and asked if he and Jordan could join them for breakfast and then meet with Carl their I.T. guy. Milo glanced at the digital clock on the nightstand. "Sure, how about in an hour? Where?" James told them to come to the penthouse. *"We want to keep a low profile. Take the private elevator. We'll leave our floor unlocked."* Milo hung up and tickled Jordan's toes. "Time to get up. We have a breakfast meeting with Kate and James in an hour." Milo called first dibs on the bathroom and Jordan rolled over for a few extra winks.

Milo loved the shower with its 10 spray heads and wondered what it would cost for them to re-work the bathroom at their condo. He dried off standing under the overhead warming lamp and slipped into one of the hotel's plush terry robes. "Jordan, it's time to get up. You have forty minutes to make yourself look awake. Hurry, breakfast with James and Kate is at nine." Jordan dragged herself to the bathroom but wasn't moving very fast. "You were on fire last night Mr. Starr I can hardly walk." Milo smiled as he dropped his robe and started to dress. "So were you, Mrs. Starr." Ten seconds later Jordan began one of her famous shower arias.

Sutton and Starr were on time for their breakfast with Kate and James. "Welcome." They entered the penthouse and were amazed at the view. "This is a fantastic location." James said they hardly ever looked out the windows. Kate poured them some coffee. "That's true. You can't wait till you have a fabulous view and then when you have that luxury you don't look at it that often. Shall we eat?" Mr. and Mrs. Starr joined Mr. and Mrs. Forbes for some terrific gourmet food. As they ate, James asked, "You think you've discovered something?" Milo showed them the app on his phone, explained its function and told them about how the app had reacted three times, so far.

Kate asked what they thought the app's reaction meant? Milo said, "I'm not sure, but I think the places where we experienced the notifications from the app are places that are overcharging customers. We have to keep looking, because there might be more." James wondered how many of the places on Kate's list they had visited so far. Jordan opened her phone and showed her electronic list to Kate. "I see you've done quite a bit." Jordan replied, "Yes, but we have a lot more to do." Kate told them that she was thankful for their help. Milo mentioned they probably had to revisit some places. "I didn't have my app open all the time. Now I will, for sure."

Milo finished his Eggs Benedict and told them how much they loved their hotel. "It's very well maintained with lots of great employees." James filled his coffee cup, "But, it seems there might be a few rotten apples in the barrel. Tell me where you've seen the app react and we'll have Carl look at the charges." Jordan smiled, "I just realized that eating here, in your penthouse, means I don't have to eat at the donut shop. That's what I had scheduled for this morning." Kate smiled, "Well, this is better, right?" Jordan nodded and raised her coffee cup and folded her napkin. "That was wonderful, thank you for inviting us." James took a phone call. "That was Carl. He's waiting for us. Shall we go?"

The foursome took the private express elevator to the locked off fourth floor. When the doors opened, Milo thought they had stepped into Mission Control at NASA. They waited behind a darkened glass partition while Milo and Jordan gawked at the number of monitors on the walls. Jordan looked at her partner, "I know you love this, but close your mouth." Milo did love it and realized that with so many cameras around the hotel it would be almost impossible for someone to pull a scam, and yet it was happening. Carl opened an unmarked side door and James motioned for everyone to enter the private office.

"Carl, this is Milo Starr and Jordan Sutton." Carl shook hands with the P.I. pair. "I know you folks. I've been following you since you arrived. You've been busy." Jordan smiled, "Yes we have, but we have a lot more to do." James asked Milo to explain what they had found so far. Milo showed Carl his app and explained what happened at two locations in the hotel. Carl didn't know about the app. He didn't have a scanner account, so he never had an occasion to use something like that. Milo told him that in their business, using a scanner was almost a daily occurrence. "You never know when you're being recorded." Jordan was looking at the super high-tech room. "Do all hotels have this many computers and cameras?" Carl replied, "Some have more. Let's look at the two places where your app spiked." Carl used the office computer to access the Pub cameras. "Here's the Pub, is that the bartender?" "No, it was a guy named Tim." Carl made a note to put the Pub on the watch list.

Milo continued, "The other place is El Oro Mexicana which, by the way, has the best Mexican food we've ever had." James and Kate smiled at that comment. Carl punched up the three cameras in that establishment. "It happened at the bar, right?" Milo told him it was a male employee, but they didn't know his name. Carl made a note to watch this bar too. Milo asked how Carl first discovered the erroneous charges.

"We were contacted by clients from Boston who noticed the extra charges on their credit card statements." Milo asked where the charges came from?

Carl brought up the first statement on his computer. Milo looked at the statement and saw five highlighted charges. "You're sure these aren't real?" Carl assured him that the clients weren't trying to cheat them. "It's not that much money they just wanted to alert us to the mistake." Milo asked if they could identify where the charge was made. "No, that's why we sent notes to everyone who stayed here for the past twelve months. Some responded, some didn't"

James said, "I think we've found all of the erroneous charges to date." Jordan replied, "I don't think so. What about the couple next to us at the Mexican bar last night?" Milo nodded. "Jordan's right. We saw that happen twice last evening at El Oro. Can you look at our charge statement right now?" Carl said he could. "Give me your card." Milo handed over the special credit card and after a few moments the statement displayed. James and Kate looked on but noticed that the statement wasn't up to date. "I guess we won't see your current charges for a day or two." Carl told them that he would continue to check. James asked, "Milo, do you have any new thoughts?" Starr looked out into the maze of monitors and became very quiet.

"Yes, I have an idea." Everyone turned toward Milo. "Can we do this? Put up a closed sign on the locker rooms. Say it's for a plumbing problem. Then we go into the room and scan the lockers." James asked, "What do you hope to find?" Milo told them that he thought the card scanners might be in their uniforms. If we scan the lockers, we might find out who might be guilty." James talked quietly to Kate and then picked up the phone. After the short call, he said he talked with the head of maintenance. "He said they would have the lockers closed after the next shift change in about twenty minutes."

He thanked Carl for his help, and their I.T. guy said he would be watching Jordan and Milo as they finished out their stay. "If you folks need anything else, just let me know." Sutton and Starr also thanked Carl for his time, as they headed toward the locker room with James and Kate. They took the executive elevator to the casino floor level. The doors opened, and they were greeted by Davy, the head of the maintenance department.

"Mr. & Mrs. Forbes it's good to see you. The dressing room areas are empty, and we have the closed signs in place. I put a plumbing crew on standby, just in case." James thanked Davy and asked him to wait outside. "Just make sure nobody enters." Davy nodded in agreement. He would never question Mr. Forbes. They entered the men's dressing room, and Milo began to scan the closed lockers and the dressing area. His scanner didn't flash once. "Sorry, nothing here. Can we go to the ladies changing room?"

Kate knocked on their door and hearing nothing, she opened the door. Once again Milo and Jordan looked over everything. They scanned the lockers and once again, the app didn't react. James opened the main door, and as they left, he asked what Milo thought about the response. "Well, I guess their units are disconnected when the people aren't working." They thanked Davy for his help. "You can remove the signs and open the dressing rooms. Give your plumbing crew and yourself an additional two hours overtime for today and don't mention this to anybody." Davy smiled, "Will do, and thank you Mr. Forbes."

James and Kate escorted their guests into the executive elevator. "We'll keep looking and call you if we find any new leads." They thanked James and Kate for breakfast and the tour and headed for their suite. Once inside, Jordan called their extremely obnoxious client, Kristy Merrill. Jordan explained that they did have a lead on the painting and their contact asked about the reward. "How much do they want?" Jordan told her, "Twelve-hundred dollars." Ms. Merrill agreed instantly. Jordan told her they were out of town on a case, but if she deposited the reward in their online bank account, they would have a messenger pick up the painting and deliver it to her. She gave Ms. Merrill the account information and told her they would call her later in the day.

Milo was entering data on his phone when Jordan joined him in the living room area of the suite. "Kristy Merrill said yes to the twelve-hundred bucks." Milo looked up and laughed, "I knew she would. The painting is worth about two million." Jordan sat, not believing what she just heard. "Two-million?" "Milo grinned at his partner, "Yes, it's a Kandinsky. He was a very famous Russian painter." Jordan couldn't believe it. Milo's cell phone received a text alert. "Someone just posted twelve-hundred dollars to our online account." "That would be from Kristy. I'll call Baldy and set up the delivery." Milo stopped her. "Don't mention the value of the painting. We'll just give him his reward." Jordan laughed, "You're right, if he knew about that, he'd want a lot more."

Milo was trying to get their expenditures up to date when Carol called. "Yes, we're fine." She wanted to know when they would be back, "You've got about ten new clients to call." Milo told her they were still on this stakeout. "We'll be back soon." Jordan interrupted his work to tell him that Baldy would wrap the painting and have it delivered by messenger to Ms. Merrill ASAP. "I told him we'd pick up the cost of the messenger and we'd send the reward once the client had the painting." Milo was happy that the case was finished. "Let's get out of here. We've got places to go and money to spend." Jordan checked her makeup, flipped her hair, grabbed her bag and said, "Let's go. Time to play Keno and eat." Milo said, "Eat? Again?"

CHAPTER 11

You Owe Me a Ring

Sutton and Starr decided on a quick bite in the food court. Milo walked all around the area pretending to look at the food and accepted several samples as he scanned each walk-up restaurant for electronic bugs. They were all clean. He found Jordan already eating a six-inch meatball sub which looked and smelled terrific. "There are no scanners here. Where did you get the sandwich?" Her mouth was full of sloppy goodness, so she just pointed over her shoulder. Milo zipped across the court and ordered, and while waiting for his lunch to be made, he received a call from Baldy. "Hi B-Man what's up?" Baldy said he wrapped the painting and it was just picked up by the messenger service. "I told them to text you when your client receives it."

Milo was very impressed with his old friend's attitude on this matter. "That was fast." Baldy told him to be just as fast transferring the reward money to his online cash-account when the painting was delivered. Milo assured him he'd take care of it. Jordan was happy that case was almost over. "We still have to find Tonto." Milo looked at her as if to say, "What are you talking about?" Jordan let out a sigh, "Kristy's dog, Tonto." Milo nodded. "I don't think there's much we can do about that."

He finished his meatball sub, wiped the sauce from his face and said, "I think we should head over to the Dublin Pub for a drink." Jordan agreed and handed him her food receipt as she picked up the trays. He snagged his receipt just as it was about to hit the trash. "I'll enter these at the Pub." They left the food court and started toward the bar. The casino was crowded again today. There was a lot of slot machine action. They wandered over to a very busy craps table and stood for a moment watching the excited players as they rolled the dice and placed bets. "It really looks exciting, but this isn't my game." Jordan agreed, "I'm a Keno and video poker girl." They turned to leave and bumped into a casino employee who apologized as he crossed the floor. Milo's cell phone buzzed. When he looked, the scanner app was still glowing. "Where did that guy go?" Jordan didn't know who he was talking about.

They entered the Dublin Pub and were greeted by Tim. "Welcome back, what kin I git ya today?" Milo asked for Tim's suggestion, "What is the best Irish Beer?" The tall, handsome gent smiled broadly, "That's easy, Guinness. How about a pint?" Milo said, "Sure, bring me one." "And for the lass?" Jordan asked for some white wine. Tim turned and began to get their order. Milo put his cell phone on the bar and opened the scanner app. He was inputting data about their expenditures when the drinks arrived, and his cell phone flashed. Milo stopped working and took a sip of the wonderful beer served at the perfect temperature. "Excellent." Tim smiled, "I'm glad ya like it."

Milo hugged his lady and whispered, "He set off the alarm again." She smiled and quietly said, "He set off *my* alarm as soon as we walked in. He's hot." Milo whacked her on the thigh and hugged her again. "Do you have any additional receipts?" Jordan rustled around in her purse as Milo went back to work on his phone. He opened the scanner app and set it to BLOCK SIGNAL. Milo watched Tim intently as he moved from patron to patron. Each time the bartender took a patron's credit card or room key and rubbed it on his right forearm Milo's app displayed the following notice, *"Device Off-Line."* Tim didn't seem to notice that the extra charges weren't being recorded and he continued to go about his business. Milo was satisfied with his test and he quickly removed the BLOCK.

Jordan pushed her wine glass forward. Tim asked, "Will ya be havin' another?" Milo reached for his credit card. "Not right now. We need to hit the machines." Tim took their card and swiped it on his arm. Milo added a tip, signed the check and left the bar. He hugged his make-believe wife and said, "I just took Tim's device off-line and he didn't know it wasn't working. We need to talk to Carl again." Jordan hugged him back, and as they settled into the Keno lounge, she said, "I didn't notice anything out of the ordinary." Milo smiled and said, "Tim had no idea his scanner wasn't working," as he sent a text to James asking when they could meet with Carl.

Jordan kept playing game after game in the very well-appointed Keno lounge. She would win a game and then play again. Milo was having fun just watching her pick numbers. She asked him for a number or two, and they were winning a little. As long as they kept playing, the cocktail girls kept plying them with booze. Milo was having a great time. He received a text from James saying that Carl was gone for the day. ***"How about first thing tomorrow?"*** He wrote back telling James to call them when Carl would be available. He leaned over to Jordan as she was marking her ticket. "I have an idea that I want to run by you." Jordan got up, "Hold that thought, I have to play this combination." Milo laughed, finished his drink and waited for his non-gambling partner to return.

She rejoined him with a fan of bills. Milo laughed at her fan dance. "For someone who doesn't gamble you sure are playing a lot." She leaned over towards him and flipped the bills in his face, "And winning a lot too. We have to keep up appearances." She was right. Milo picked up a Keno ticket and a black crayon and began to make his marks. "Here's what I have in mind. Since I was able to take Tim's device offline, how about setting up a permanent blocking device in the Dublin Pub?" Jordan looked at him and wanted to know more. "We rig the device, so it only affects the bar area, not their point-of-sale machines. We don't want the hotel to lose money, only the cheats." Jordan took their slips and started toward the Keno counter. "What does that accomplish?"

Milo looked around, "Well, if it happens enough Tim and others might call somebody for a repair. Then we remove the block before they arrive and put it back once they are gone." Jordan placed their bets. "That could work." Milo took his ticket and smiled, "Plus it might get cutie Tim in trouble."

Milo hit a Keno jackpot on the only ticket he played. He won two-thousand dollars. Jordan was very happy and asked, "What are you planning to do with that money?" Milo grinned back at her. "I don't know. I might buy my girlfriend a present. Don't tell her because I don't want to spoil the surprise." Jordan whacked him on the upper arm with her Keno crayon. He pulled her close and whispered, "Just tell me what you want, and it's yours." Jordan sat back in the comfortable chair and said, "Let me think about that." She filled out a new ticket and held out her left hand. She flashed the diamonds in Milo's face, "I want a nice ring like this one." Milo almost choked on his gin and tonic. "A wedding ring?"

Jordan leaned over and kissed her partner on the cheek. "Not a wedding ring just a nice-looking gift from the man I love." Milo smiled broadly and kissed his lady sweetly on the lips. "You really know how to get what you want, don't you? Let's go." Jordan picked up her tickets, "Where?" Milo put his arm around her shoulders, "First, a stop at a store on Rodeo Drive North and then a dip in our private spa." Jordan pulled him along. "Let's hurry. I don't want you to change your mind." It didn't take them long to arrive at the shopping/dining area of the hotel known as RDN, which is short for Rodeo Drive North. It was a perfect recreation of the famed Beverly Hills shopping district complete with all the fancy names. Milo opened the door to the very exclusive RDN Diamonds. "After you Madam."

Jordan began to ooh and aah as she looked at the shiny baubles. Milo's phone rang. He told her to keep looking as he took a call from Carol. He told her all was going well. "I think we'll be back in two or three days." They chatted for a few moments, but the call was interrupted by a text from James Forbes. "Carol we'll call you later today."

Milo looked at the text. *"We see you're in the jewelry store. Kate wants to buy Jordan a present. Get her a pretty necklace".* Milo looked up at the in-store camera and nodded YES. He showed Jordan the text. She looked at the camera, smiled and asked to see the diamond and onyx necklace. She tried it on and moved to the mirror in front of the in-store camera. Milo got a text from Kate, *"Perfect choice!"* Milo showed his phone to Jordan. "I love this piece. Can we buy it?" Milo said yes as he handed over his special credit card. He watched his scanner app. No reaction. The clerk was very happy to have made such a high-end sale. She put the necklace in a very swanky purple box with a satin lining, wrapped it in shiny white paper and placed it in a small RDN Diamonds logo bag. The app didn't react. "Thank you for shopping with us." Jordan smiled as she raised the bag to the surveillance camera. She turned to Milo. "Thank you, we're off to the spa, but you still owe me a ring."

CHAPTER 12

Too Many Restaurants

Jordan and Milo decided to slip into the private spa adjacent to their expansive bathroom. It had been a very long time since they felt so relaxed and they wanted to enjoy this moment. The hot water bubbling against their skin put them in a very romantic mood. Jordan floated over to her aroused partner and kissed him sweetly as he smiled and stroked her semi-wet hair. "I don't know why I get so excited each time I see you like this." Jordan batted her eyes and whispered, "I know why," as she moved her hands below the water line. "It's because I'm super-hot and you're super-horny." Their intimate moment was destroyed by a ringing phone. Milo stretched over Jordan to look at the caller I.D. on his cell phone. "It's Carol, I have to take it, or she'll think we've been kidnapped."

"Hi Carol, we're fine, thanks for checking. Anything we have to take care of now?" Carol replied, "Nothing that can't wait. Any idea when you'll be back? I'm going crazy sitting around the house. I miss you guys." Milo was trying to sound normal and not overly excited which was almost impossible because Jordan kept kissing him all over. "You sound out of breath, are you okay?" Milo assured her that he was fine. Carol told him they received a check for three-thousand dollars from Kristy Merrill. Milo seemed confused and asked, "Three Thousand?" Carol read the note, *"I doubled your fee because Tonto came home too. He picked up a girlfriend along the way.* It's signed Kristy. She dotted the 'i' with a little heart. Does that make sense to you?" Milo laughed and told her it made perfect sense. "See you soon."

Jordan hugged her favorite guy and asked about the three grand. Milo explained as he watched her pick up an oversized towel and head for the shower. "That's it? You're finished?" Jordan glanced over her shoulder as she moved to the bathroom. "Yep, finished for now, we have to eat again." Milo settled back in the warm water. "Eat, again?" Jordan opened the bathroom door and said, "We still have four restaurants and nine shops to visit." Milo hit the super jet button on the spa and settled back for a few moments of water massage. It was a perfect moment because the spa bubbles drowned out Jordan's version of some pop song he didn't recognize.

With more food to eat and more shopping to do, they were in for another busy day at the hotel. Milo put his cell phone on the table at the Chinese restaurant. It flashed when their server approached with menus. The charming young lady said, "I'll be right back with your tea." He showed Jordan his flashing cell. Jordan ordered and had to rap Milo with the menu as he seemed deep in thought. He snapped out of it and said, "I'll have the same." Jordan sipped her tea and quietly asked, "What's on your mind?" "We're not finished with this job. We have to go back to all the places on the list that we visited before we went into the Dublin Pub." Jordan nodded and said, "You're right. They might all be in on this." Jordan showed him her list of every place they visited complete with the dates, times and what they spent. Milo was impressed, "Very nice work Mrs. Starr."

They sat quietly, thinking as they waited for their food. The flashing cell app caught Milo's attention. He looked up to see a different young lady pushing a dim sum cart. "You want dim sum?" They both declined. The cart passed, and his phone stopped flashing. Their food arrived, and after a few bites, Milo smiled at Jordan. "I've got an idea. It's strange but stay with me on this." She put down her chopsticks. "What, a strange idea from you? I don't believe it!"

Milo looked around and quietly explained what he was thinking. "What if all of us confront Tim in the Pub, since we know he's involved for sure? What do you think?" She thought if James and Kate were with them, it might work. "We tell him we know what's going on and see if he knows who's running the operation." Jordan smirked at his idea. "So, he'll just blurt out the answers? I don't think so." Milo picked up a chopstick. "Maybe not, but this is a crime, and he and the other people who are involved could end up in jail." Jordan picked up her chopstick and crossed swords, so-to-speak, with Milo. "OK, when you put it that way, it might work. Let's eat and call James."

They finished the delicious Chinese food and put the special credit card on the table. The waitress picked up their credit card, and as she walked away, she rubbed the card across her right forearm. Milo watched and made a note on his phone about the action and the time. They exited the Chinese restaurant and immediately called James. Mr. Forbes listened and said, "Milo, if it's that widespread I think talking to the bartender in private is the way to go. I'll have Carl check to see when he will be on his shift." Milo asked. "When will you and Kate be back here?" James said they were planning to fly up in the morning. "We'll call you when we arrive." Milo said he'd wait for their call.

He relayed the conversation to Jordan who was looking at her list. "We still have to buy some homemade designer soap, a few cigars, a watch and you have to pick up some shaving products. That's today. Tomorrow we have another list." Milo asked if they could go back to the buffet where they ate on the first day. Jordan said, "Okay that will be dinner tonight. But we still haven't been to the steakhouse, the prime rib place or the bar-b-que restaurant." Milo smiled, "Maybe that's for the next trip? What about bars, have we hit every one of them?" Jordan checked her master list and counted. "No, we still have five to go." Milo grabbed her arm. "Guide me to one of them. Let's make it only four to go." Jordan looked at the hotel map on her phone and whirled him around. "We're going this way."

It was only a short walk to a small bar in the middle of the bustling casino. They pulled up two barstools and waited as the busy bartender acknowledged their presence. "I'll be there in a moment." Milo looked around and realized that the casino was doing good business in the early afternoon. "This place must make a fortune." The bartender put napkins in front of them and asked, "What would you like?" Jordan said, "A margarita for me with salt, Milo?" Mr. Starr put his phone on the bar, and it flashed as he said, "A Bloody Mary, please." The bartender smiled and began to make their drinks. Milo pointed to the flashing app. He made a note on his phone about this location.

Jordan loved her drink. "It's not as good as the ones at Margo-Rita's, but it's good." Milo liked his drink as well. "What are we doing this afternoon?" "We're shopping and then going to the buffet, but first we're going to play Keno for a while."

CHAPTER 13

Confrontation

Jordan was a small winner at Keno again and dinner at the buffet was fantastic. Milo walked all over the buffet with his phone and didn't get a flash anywhere. "I guess this place is clear." Jordan smiled, "That's good to know." Milo liked what Jordan was having for dessert. "That looks wonderful, what is it?" She offered him a bite, "It's Key Lime Pie." He left to get a piece. As Jordan was finishing her dessert, the head cashier walked past their table and the phone flashed. Jordan kept an eye on the older woman and when Milo returned she pointed out the lady. "So, it really is happening everywhere. James might have to fire his entire staff." Milo made a note about the buffet and turned his phone list to Jordan. "The list keeps getting longer." They finished, left a tip on the table and Jordan put the receipt in her purse.

As they walked up the hallway toward the casino, Jordan pulled Milo's arm. "You know what we haven't been doing Mr. Starr?" He looked at her and didn't have a clue. She put her hand on the back of his neck and gave him a "very-married kiss". "That's what we haven't been doing. We're not acting like a newlywed couple." Milo gave her a quick kiss on the cheek and smiled, "You're right Mrs. Starr, let's not let that happen again." They reached the end of the corridor and Milo noticed the small, yet trendy Corner Bar. "Is this place on our list?" Jordan opened her phone and checked. "Yes, it is, and we haven't been there yet."

Milo took her arm. "Well, Mrs. Starr how about an after-dinner drink?" They found two bar stools and looked around. The place wasn't very crowded. The female bartender said, "What can I get for you?" Milo ordered a gin and tonic, and Jordan wanted some white wine. "I'll be back in a moment." Milo quietly noted that she didn't have any sleeves, so he didn't think she was over-charging. He put his phone on the bar and made a note that they were at the Corner Bar. Jordan whispered in his ear, "Have you been keeping track of everything we've spent?" He whispered back and added a kiss on her cheek. "Yes, take a look."

Milo showed Jordan the account screen, and as she read, their drinks arrived and the scanner app flashed. She handed the phone over to Milo. They toasted each other, and Milo said, "She must have the scanner in her bloomers." Jordan laughed, "Only you would say the word bloomers. Anybody else would have said ass." Milo looked around again and snapped a photo of the bartender. "What would you like to do tonight?" Jordan knew exactly what she wanted to do. "I want to go drinking and dancing." Milo thought that was a great idea. He handed his credit card to the bartender who swiped it on her short skirt on the way to the cash register. Milo folded the receipt and put a tip on the bar.

Jordan stopped at the Keno lounge and bought fifty games. "This way I won't miss anything while we're dancing. I can check the tickets later." They could hear the cover band already performing as they approached the club. They entered the darkened Golden Note Lounge and Jordan found them a small table with comfortable chairs toward the rear of the club. She checked this club off her list as Milo put his cell on the table. Their waitress approached. "Hi, I'm Jessica, what can I get you?"

It was hard to hear, so the waitress leaned in to get the order. The app flashed as Jordan ordered a white wine and Milo wanted a lite draft beer. The girl left, and the flashing stopped. Milo continued to enter the data as his phone flashed again. He looked up as another waitress passed behind them heading to the next table. Then another flash as someone crossed behind them again. He leaned over to Jordan, kissed her on the cheek and said, "It seems everybody working in this club has a scanner." Milo finished his entries and put the phone in his jacket pocket.

The drinks arrived as the band began one of Jordan's favorites. Milo thanked their waitress and put napkins on top of both drinks because Jordan wanted to dance. He danced and kept his eyes on their drinks. Meanwhile, in his jacket pocket, the app was flashing and buzzing quietly each time a waiter or waitress crossed near them. The dance ended, and they made their way back to their table. "That was fun. Thank you 'husband' of mine."

The older couple at the next table smiled and asked how long they had been married? Jordan said, "Just a few weeks." The wife smiled at them, "We've been married for thirty-five years. Today is our anniversary." Milo raised his glass, "Congratulations, may we buy you a drink?" The husband nodded, "Yes, thank you."

Milo motioned to Jessica who leaned way over so she could hear the order and Milo could see her ample chest. He felt his phone buzzing inside his pocket. "We'd like to buy these folks a drink. Please add it to our check." "Will do, sweetie." She left, and Milo's phone calmed down. Jordan glared at him and smacked his arm. "Nice way to take orders. I'll bet her boobs improve her tips." Milo pretended not to hear her. He said his phone had been buzzing all over this place.

He excused himself and made his way among the tables. His phone buzzed at least ten times on the way to the men's room. On the way back to their table, he took a different route and once again the phone went crazy. He told Jordan and marked this club as ground zero, with a happy face. They danced a few more times, said goodnight to the anniversary couple, settled the check with Jessica and left the club. "What would you like to do Mrs. Starr?" "That's easy, check my Keno games and then ravage you." Milo loved her answer as he picked up the pace.

The phone and the sunlight through the crack in the blackout drapes awakened Milo at the same time. "Good morning Milo, this is James. We just landed. Can we meet in my office in about two hours?" Milo said they would be there. He hung up the phone and rolled over to kiss his sleeping beauty on the neck.

"Time to get up lover. James and Kate want to meet with us in about two hours." Jordan grunted and mumbled something about Milo going first. Milo took the hint and started his day with a smile. "Last night was fantastic. I liked being ravaged."

They were awake, but not really, as they waited about ten minutes in the Forbes' outer office. Cassie, Mr. Forbes secretary, said that Mr. and Mrs. Forbes would be there shortly. She wasn't kidding, about two seconds later James opened the door for his wife who upon seeing Sutton and Starr said, "You guys look like you've been up all night." Milo smiled, "Well, sort-of. That's what playing married will do to you." Kate laughed and told them she understood. They entered his private office and James asked Cassie to bring in a coffee service. He and Kate wanted to know all about Jordan and Milo's time at the hotel.

Jordan started, "First, it's beautiful here. We didn't realize how big the place was. We've done just about everything on the list, but it's been hard." She showed her phone to Kate. "We still have a few restaurants to visit and a couple of things to buy. Other than that, we've been everywhere and done almost everything. Milo's put on about six pounds." James laughed, "I know the feeling. It can happen here for sure. Tell us what you've discovered so far."

Milo told them again about the app on his phone and how he'd been using it to find more incidents of possible fraudulent charges. Kate asked, "I know you found one at the Irish pub, did you find others?" Milo opened the app and scanned their office. It was clear. "The Pub is one of many that we found." He checked his notes. "So far, forty-five employees have registered on the scanner. Unfortunately, I didn't start using the app until we went to the Dublin Pub. Every place we visited before we went to the Pub has to be re-scanned."

The coffee service arrived. Kate thanked Cassie and poured as James asked, "Where do we start? It sounds bigger than we thought." Milo thanked Kate for the coffee. "I have a crazy idea and wanted to run it by both of you. I'd like us to talk with Tim the bartender at the pub, is there anyway to call him to your office?" James asked, "Call him now?" Milo explained that he wanted to ask Tim how much he knew about the operation and how long he'd been involved. James thought for a moment, "Yes, we could have Cassie call him." He hit the intercom, "Cassie can you come in for a moment?" The well-dressed assistant entered, notepad in hand. "Yes sir, what do you need?" James said, "Call the Dublin Pub and speak with a bartender named Tim." She began to make notes. "Ask him nicely to come to my office. Just tell him I'd like to have a word with him." Cassie smiled, "I'll get right on that, sir." James turned to Milo. "Ok, he'll be here, I'm sure. Then what do we do?"

Milo smiled, "That's the easy part. Yesterday, I blocked his scanner for a moment and he wasn't aware of the outage. I want to tell him that we know about what's going on and find out who got him involved. That may lead us to the person running this operation. The overcharging might seem small to a bartender or waiter but when you add it all up, it's a big-time crime. I want him to know that someone might be going to jail for this." Cassie buzzed James. "He's on his way."

Kate said, "If we get the right answers, you don't have to eat in the remaining restaurants." Milo laughed, "True, but we could return in the future and pick up where we left off."

Kate asked about the necklace. Jordan smiled and said, "I love it." "We thought it would be a nice way to remind you of your time at the hotel." The ladies continued to talk jewelry as Milo finished his coffee. Cassie knocked. "Tim Foley is here." James stood and welcomed the tall Irishman who appeared very anxious. "Tim, thank you for coming. I don't know if you've ever met my wife and partner, this is Katherine." Tim nodded to Mrs. Forbes. James continued, "This is Milo Starr and Jordan Sutton." Tim smiled and extended his hand. "Yes, they've been in the Dublin a couple of times. Did I offend ya? Is that why I'm here?" Milo handed Tim his business card. He read their job description. "You're Private Investigators?

James explained that Sutton and Starr had been hired to find out how and people were being overcharged at the hotel. Tim suddenly became very quiet. "They discovered the scanning devices." Milo cut in, "We believe you have one on your person right now." James continued, "These extra charges are costing the hotel a small fortune because we have to reimburse the customers." Tim looked at the ladies and then at James and realized that he was probably in trouble and might be out of a job. "I don't understand. I only make a few charges each day."

James said, "Tim you're not the only one doing this. It's happening all over the hotel. How long have you've been using the scanner?" Milo asked, "And who got you involved?" The Irish gent took a deep breath. "You wouldn't be recordin' this would ya?" Milo assured him they weren't. Suddenly, Tim dropped his accent. "The reason I ask is, I don't want to end up in a back alley with my throat cut open." Everyone reacted to his statement. Jordan asked, "Why did you say that?" Tim got very quiet, "I said it because I think people who've been involved in this operation have been killed." Milo asked, "You know that for a fact?" Tim shook his head, "No, I just heard things." Jordan asked, "And what happened to your accent?" He paused, smiled and continued, "I used to come to the pub years back because it was like a slice of home. Very authentic! Each time I was there to drink, I would use my accent. One of the bartenders said he was leaving and I asked him how to apply and I got the job. My accent is authentic, but I don't have to use it all the time." He looked around the room. "When Leroy, the former Food and Beverage Manager approached me with the scanner idea, I figured it was only a few charges, so what harm could there be? Now you tell me there are hundreds of extra charges every day. I only do it a few times each shift."

Jordan looked at the handsome Irish gent, "Credit card fraud is a crime. Someone will be going to jail for this, I hope it's not you." Tim realized that he was caught and talking might be the way out of all of this. "Mr. Forbes, I make a decent salary and get good tips but with a wife and child at home, I could always use a little more. About a year ago, Leroy inquired about my life and expenses. I thought I was gettin' a raise. He showed me the device." Tim unbuttoned his right sleeve and exposed the portable scanner clipped to his forearm. "Charlie explained how it worked and told me that each time I scanned a guest's card I would make a buck per charge."

Milo asked if Tim knew anyone else in the operation. "No, only the Food and Beverage manager." Kate wanted to know how many employees were doing this. "I don't know ma'am, I've never asked anybody or mentioned it to anyone." He looked at everyone in the room. "Until this meeting, I thought I was the only one doing it."

Milo had a strange thought. "Tim, has the system ever stopped or locked up?" "Yes, it did once for about an hour." James asked how it got resolved. Tim explained, "Out of the blue, a repair guy showed up, tweaked a few things and it started workin' again." Milo looked at the device. "Tim if you shut it off during your shift, how long would it take someone to come and fix it?" Tim told them it took about twenty to thirty minutes the last time it happened. "Would you be willing to shut it off tomorrow?" Tim said, "Yes, if that would help." Milo told him, "When you see us enter the Pub tomorrow, just turn it off, and let's see what happens."

James told Tim not to contact the Food and Beverage Manager. "Just go about your business as you do every day. We'll see you tomorrow." Tim stood and thanked them for helping him in this situation. "I've wanted to quit but Charlie said the people who were running this show didn't like quitters. That kind of scared me, so, I stayed." Kate put her hand on his arm,

"Tim, we understand." He nodded and quietly headed back to the Pub.

When they were alone, James thanked Sutton and Starr for their help so far. "It sounds like the people who are involved are being forced to use the scanners." Milo agreed and said, "Let's meet at the pub around noon tomorrow, turn off the system, and see what happens." Kate asked if they would like to join them for dinner. "How about one of the restaurants you haven't been able to try?" Jordan looked at Milo's list. "We haven't been to the steakhouse, the bar-b-que place or the prime rib restaurant." Kate looked at the guys. Milo said, "How about the steakhouse. I heard it was the best in town." James smiled and told them, "It *is* the best. We'll see you there at seven, okay?"

Milo and Jordan left the office with a sense of accomplishment. They talked as they walked to the central gaming concourse. "Let's hope Tim keeps his mouth shut." Jordan said, "I think he will. He seemed scared stiff at the possibility of doing time." Milo looked around the massive casino and asked, "Well, Mrs. Starr, what's your pleasure?" Jordan said, "Video Poker."

CHAPTER 14

The Dublin Pub

Milo glanced at his watch, it was just after noon. He ordered two pints of Guinness and waited at the bar for the order to be filled. Tim pushed the two frosted glasses forward and asked, "When do you want me to disconnect? Milo told him, "We'll do it as soon as Mr. and Mrs. Forbes arrive." Tim nervously went back to work, and Milo carried both glasses to their table in the corner without spilling a drop. Jordan took her glass and commented, "You did that very well. I think you have a future in food service." They tasted the Pub's finest while they waited for James and Kate.

Milo caught a glimpse of the owners a moment before they stepped into the bar. He nodded to Tim who turned toward the cash register and disengaged his scanning device. Jordan welcomed James and Kate and asked if they wanted anything from the bar. Kate said, "I would love some iced tea." Milo headed to the bar and placed the order. Tim told Milo that he was nervous about not having his device connected. Milo smiled and told him not to worry. "You're not in any trouble." When he brought their order to the table, once again not spilling a drop, Kate joked that Milo would make a fantastic waiter. Jordan toasted her and smiled, "That's funny since I just told him the same thing." Milo made a face at Jordan and took a sip of his beer.

James wanted to know how much they had spent so far. Milo checked his phone and showed James the accounting. He looked it over and said, "Milo, you haven't been spending very much, have you?" Jordan thought they had. "We've been to almost every restaurant and shop in the hotel, Milo even had a mani-pedi." James laughed, "Just kidding with you. The account looks fine." They continued to chit-chat for about fifteen minutes, but stopped when a man wearing dark blue work clothes entered. Tim stopped wiping down the bar, looked toward the table in the corner and nodded. Milo put his cell phone on the table with the scanner app set to BLOCK SIGNAL.

Everyone watched as the workman stepped behind the bar, opened his shoulder satchel and put a small laptop next to the point-of-sale computer system. Milo was about to head to the bar when a short, stout man entered and walked quickly toward Tim. James whispered, "That's our Food and Beverage Manager, Charlie Brady." He seemed agitated as he spoke to the bartender who appeared to be very nervous. Charlie slammed his hand on the bar and said something in anger to Tim. The workman was attempting to re-connect the system, but it still wasn't working. The technician didn't understand why the system wasn't working. He stopped, closed his small laptop and spoke to Charlie who nodded as the workman left the bar.

The Food and Beverage Manager turned to leave and stopped dead in his tracks when he saw James Forbes. Charlie immediately walked over to the corner table. "Mr. Forbes nice to see you." "Charlie, this is my wife Katherine and my friends Milo Starr and Jordan Sutton." The Food & Beverage Manager acknowledged everyone and seemed a little uneasy. "What brings you to the Dublin, Charlie?" "We're having a little trouble with our credit card system."

James stood and his 6ft 2in height towered over Charlie. "We know about the trouble. We caused it." Milo stood and pulled out a chair. Charlie sat and looked at James. "What do you mean you caused the trouble?" James said, "This is Milo Starr, he'll tell you what's going on." James motioned to Milo who immediately began to explain about discovering that Tim and a multitude of employees were using the personal credit card skimmers. Charlie didn't say a word. He just looked at James and then the others at the table expressionless. Kate asked. "How long have the scanners been in use?" Charlie lowered his voice. "Should we go somewhere more private?" Milo checked his scanner. It was GREEN. He showed it to Charlie and James. "I'm blocking all devices. We can talk here."

Charlie picked up a bar napkin and wiped his brow. "You promoted me about eight months ago. That's when Leroy, ah…died." James remembered, and added to the story for Sutton and Starr. "Leroy Powers had been here for a long time. He worked for my father. We all took his death very hard." Charlie looked at Milo, "That's how I got promoted. I took over Leroy's job and his office and didn't know anything about the scanners when I started. I had been an assistant in the F & B department for about five years." Milo stopped him, "In all that time, you never had an inkling of what was going on?" Charlie shook his head. "No. None of the staff talked to me about it." Jordan asked, "When was the first time you learned about the scanning devices?"

Charlie thought for a moment, "I learned about the charge system number two when we had a malfunction." He motioned for Tim to come over to the table. "Tim, when was the first time that the charge system got messed up here?" Tim quickly said, "That was about two or three months ago, I think." Charlie thanked the bartender who headed back to work, and he continued to explain, "Well, that's when I found out about what was going on." James wondered, "Why didn't you report it to the General Manager or to my office?"

Charlie looked at Milo. "Are you sure it's safe to talk here?" Milo assured him it was. Charlie took a deep breath and then said, "When that happened for the first time, the workman fixed the system and stopped by my office for me to sign his work order. I looked at the charge which said it was for repair of CC system number two. I didn't know what that was, so I questioned him about it. He said he understood that I was new on the job and he would have his boss drop by to explain everything to me, so I signed the form. As I was leaving my office the next evening, a rather large, well-dressed guy stopped by to discuss the CC system number two. That's when I became aware of the operation. I told him that I didn't like the concept because I didn't like breaking the law."

Jordan could see that Charlie was having a hard time relaying the story. She handed him another napkin. He once again, wiped his brow. "I don't know the guy's name, but he told me in no uncertain terms that if I didn't keep the operation in place, my wife Dorothy, he knew her name, and our two kids would be celebrating holidays without me because I'd end up like my former boss, Leroy." James explained that Leroy, their Food and Beverage Manager, was found shot to death in the parking garage. Charlie said, "Knowing what happened to him, I wasn't about to cross these people, so I just let everything continue."

James asked if he ever got paid for doing this. "Yeah, they gave me a hundred-thousand-dollars right after the guy visited me. They said there would be another payment like that each year." Milo wanted to know what he did with the money. "I didn't spend one dime of it. I put it in a savings account and haven't touched it since." Charlie looked around the table. "What do I do now?" James told him to just keep doing what he was doing. "As far as you're concerned, nothing has changed." Charlie took a deep breath. "I'm not fired?" Kate said, "No, you're not fired. We'll figure something out." James told him to go back to work as if nothing had happened. Charlie left smiling and relieved. Milo told Tim to keep doing business as usual. "Keep your scanner on. We'll be in touch."

The foursome sat at the table looking at each other. "Milo, do you have any ideas?" Milo smiled and removed the BLOCK from the area, "James, I'm good, but not that good. I have to sit, drink and think for a while. Jordan and I will kick things around and I'll call you as soon as I have a battle plan." Kate hugged Jordan and Milo and thanked them for their help. "We're going upstairs for a while. How about you guys?" Milo told them they were heading to the Keno lounge. "It's the perfect place to sit, drink and think.

CHAPTER 15

Milo's Lucky Day

Milo was filling out a Keno slip and thinking, when a cocktail waitress asked if he would like a drink. He asked for a 7 & 7. Jordan didn't want anything. The young lady smiled and left to get his order. Milo finished marking his play slip, this time with six numbers and handed it to Jordan with a five-dollar bill. "I'm playing five bucks this time." She wished him a half-hearted "good luck" as she approached the Keno desk. The waitress returned without his drink. "I'm sorry sir, the bar is out of your whiskey. They told Food and Beverage to order some. Can I get you something else?" Milo said, "Gin and Tonic with lime and tell me where the Food and Beverage Department is, I'd like to say hi to Charlie Brady." The girl pointed to a set of double doors across the casino. "It's right through those doors. I'll be back with your drink in a moment." She crossed paths with Jordan who found Milo smiling.

"Ok, what's up? Did you make a date with that cute waitress while I was gone?" Milo dragged Jordan into her chair. "No, I found out that Charlie's office is just beyond those doors." Jordan shrugged her shoulders as the Keno balls began to fly around in the large plastic chamber. "So? His office is over there, so what?" Milo looked at his ticket as the balls were selected by the Keno machine. "I'll tell you after this game, I already have four, no five numbers." He watched as the balls continued to be selected. The Keno caller said, "Your final number is sixty-two." Milo sat up in his chair. "I can't believe it. Look, I have six out of six." Jordan checked the ticket. "Yes, you do. What did you win?"

They both moved quickly to the Keno desk. Jordan won two-dollars and Milo won seven-thousand-five-hundred. The Keno lady was smiling as she printed the receipt for the cashier's cage. "You better keep playing. This is your lucky day!" Milo asked Jordan if she had their "mad money" from Kate. She opened her purse and Milo snagged a one-hundred-dollar bill and handed it to the Keno operator. "This is for you." He took Jordan's arm and they headed for the cage. While they waited in line Jordan hugged him and whispered, "You used our mad money for that tip. You are so cheap. You've won almost ten-thousand so far. Remember, you owe me a ring." Milo was smiling as they reached the cage. The attendant asked them to step to the side to a more private area.

"How would you like this?" Milo said, "All large will be fine." The lady put a stack of fresh bills in the auto-counter, set the number at 75 and pushed start. The machine quickly counted the money. She then counted out everything by hand as they watched. She put the cash in an envelope and asked Milo to fill out an IRS form. "You have to complete this when you win more than fifteen-hundred at Keno. But you get to deduct the amount you spent for the ticket." Milo laughed as he wrote, "$7,495.00" on the line marked winning amount. He filled in everything and turned the form back to the cashier. She looked and said, "Not bad for a five-dollar investment. You know if you'd won this much or any large amount at Baccarat or any table game, you wouldn't have to fill out this form." They thanked her for the information. Jordan asked, "Where to?" Milo took her by the arm and they headed for the Food and Beverage Department.

They entered the double doors and in the first office on the right they saw Charlie Brady. "Mr. Brady, may we have a word with you?" Charlie looked up, "Come in please, I remember your name is Jordan, but ah…She's Jordan Sutton and I'm Milo Starr. Here's our card." "You're private Investigators?" "Yes, we've been hired by the owners to investigate the massive credit card over-billing going on in the hotel."

Charlie, thinking that he might soon be out of a job, was being very cooperative. He wanted to know how they caught on to the personal card scanners. Milo was about to tell Charlie about his cell phone app when it began to flash. He showed the phone to Jordan and she motioned to Charlie to be quiet. Milo began to scan the office. She started making small talk. "Charlie this is a very crowded workspace." He didn't say anything, so Jordan encouraged him to talk. "Yes, I've been meaning to put away all the files, but I always run out of time." Milo pointed to an award behind the desk and told Jordan to keep talking. She asked, "Where's a good place to eat here at the hotel? I'm hungry." Charlie started talking about several of the restaurants as Milo found another listening device behind a framed certificate of excellence awarded to Charlie and he located a bug in the phone. He finished and said, "Can we take you out to lunch?" Jordan nodded "yes," and Charlie said, "Sure, I never turn down free food." They left the office and a moment later they were in the noisy casino.

They entered a small sandwich shop and found an empty table. Milo set his phone to BLOCK SIGNALS. "This is a secure area. We can talk now." Charlie asked, "What's going on?" Milo said quietly, "Your office has two listening devices. One bug is in the base of the award behind your desk and another is attached to a certificate on the wall. Someone is tapping into your office phone line too." Charlie seemed stunned and didn't say a word. He just looked at Milo and Jordan. "So, they must know everything that's going on." Milo said, "Yes, and now they know about us too." Jordan realized that they introduced themselves to Charlie. "You're right. But who are *they*?" Charlie explained the details of the operation from his perspective.

"We have about seventy-five people all over the hotel who use the card scanners. They activate them at the top of their shift and turn them off when they clock out. I told each of them not to mention anything to anybody but I'm sure some of them know that others are doing it too." Milo asked, "How did it start?" Charlie didn't know. "It was already in place when I was promoted after Leroy was murdered." Jordan asked, "Do you know other details about Leroy's death?" Charlie looked at Jordan and hoped he wouldn't scare her. "They found him in our parking garage. He had been shot twice, once in the chest and another in the back of his head." Jordan didn't bat an eye. "Here's what they said to me. You keep things in place as they are, you'll make money and you won't end up like Leroy." Milo jumped in, "Who said that to you?" Charlie didn't know. "It was just a voice on the phone."

Then Charlie dropped a bombshell on them. "I'm just a small cog in this operation. We hired a bartender about a month ago who had worked for two different hotels on the strip. The first thing he asked me was if we were double scanning. I was shocked and learned that they were doing the same thing at both of his other jobs. He came over here because he heard we paid better." Milo and Jordan couldn't believe what they just heard.

Milo said, "What you're telling us is that at least three hotels are involved." Charlie added, "And maybe more." Jordan asked, "Have you ever told anybody about the other hotels?" Charlie quietly said, "Why would I do that? I'm not crazy, I want to keep breathing. I better get back to work. Is there anything else you need from me?" Milo told him to watch what he said in the office. "The bugs have to stay in place for now." Charlie thanked them and hoped they would put in a good word with the boss. They assured him they would. Milo and Jordan sat quietly for a moment and Jordan looked at the list on her phone. "This is one of the places we were supposed to visit. Let's eat." She headed toward the counter and ordered two sliced turkey subs with cranberry sauce, stuffing and gravy. Milo called James. He checked his app and it was still in the BLOCK MODE. "James, this is Milo. We just had a long talk with Charlie. Can we come up to your place in a half-hour?" James told them that Kate was out shopping. "I'll get her back here in thirty. See you then."

Milo finished the call and Jordan put their sandwiches on the table. "These look delicious." Jordan looked at the sign on the counter, "It's their 365 day a year holiday treat. I guess that means they always have it." Milo liked the crazy sandwich. "Don't take forever to eat. We're meeting James and Kate in a half-hour." Jordan had taken one bite when she realized something. "Milo, do you think we're getting too involved in this mess?" Milo checked the BLOCKING app. "Well, after talking to Charlie, I would say, yes. This thing is massive and if it comes crumbling down, a lot of people will lose their jobs and maybe their lives. Let's lay it all out for James and Kate and see what they say."

Jordan worked on her sloppy turkey sandwich and shook her head. Milo was also a mess as he asked, "What's wrong?" She stopped eating and laughed, "You have Thanksgiving dinner all over your face. Not a very attractive look for a honeymooner." She held up her make-believe wedding ring. Milo took her hand. She gave him a gravy kiss on the cheek and wiped some cranberry sauce from his chin as they finished lunch. "Here's the receipt. Let's go."

CHAPTER 16

Meeting in the Penthouse

James greeted Jordan and Milo. "You beat Kate back, she's still shopping. Please, make yourselves comfortable, she won't be long. Would you like coffee or a drink? My bar is open." Jordan said, "I think it's too early for my partner to start drinking." She was happy just looking at the view. Kate arrived with several shopping bags, "I found some wonderful things on sale." She turned and noticed their guests. "Hi everybody, I didn't know you were coming." James frowned at his lovely partner, "I tried to call you, but you didn't have your phone on." Kate put her bags in the foyer and admitted she didn't have her phone, "It's charging. What's up, Milo? Do you have some news for us?"

Milo and Jordan told them what they found in Charlie's office and they relayed what he told them about the operation, the employees, the other hotels involved and why he couldn't stop. "We think the people behind all of this murdered Leroy to send a message." James said he always thought it was just a mugging gone bad. "I didn't know that his death was connected to this." Kate said, "Why would you? We didn't know any of this was going on when Leroy died." James agreed as he turned toward his bar. "The bar is really open now." He poured himself a shot of double malt Scotch.

"Milo, you're telling us that we're not the only hotel involved, and nobody knows who is running this operation?" Milo nodded, "That's what we're saying." Jordan added, "And the person responsible for bugging Charlie's office knows we're involved, because we identified ourselves while we were there before Milo discovered the listening devices." Kate was suddenly very concerned. "Both of you might be in danger because of this?" Milo replied, "It's possible." James offered them a drink again and this time Milo said, "Yes." James joined his wife who was very quiet, as he asked, "How do we bring this all to an end?" Milo assured them that it was possible to stop everything. "We just have to dream up a way to do it and keep everybody safe."

Kate asked if they thought their trip to the hotel was coming to an end. Milo told them he didn't think there was anything else to be learned. "Now we have to figure out who is running this illegal operation, and stop them." James put his empty glass down on the coffee table. "You sound convinced that we can end this?" "Yes, I am." Jordan looked at Kate and said, "We'll continue to work on everything back in L.A. You guys should stay alert and be aware of your surroundings." Kate looked at James, "You mean we might be followed?" Jordan said, "We don't know for sure so. just be careful." Milo asked, "Did Charlie tell us how he was paid?" James didn't think so.

Milo looked in his pocket for Charlie's business card. "I'm going to call him." His call went directly to voicemail. Milo left no message. "Jordan, let's go see him in person." They thanked James and Kate for taking time to meet them. Kate asked if they had been to every restaurant on the original list. Jordan checked her phone and said, "Not all of them." Kate told her, "Don't miss the Pizzeria, it's the best. You should go before you leave." James said, "Join us there tonight at seven." Milo opened the door for Jordan. "Okay, we'll see you then."

Milo and Jordan hopped on the elevator and descended to the casino level. They entered the double doors, saw Charlie in his office and motioned for him to join them outside. As they walked through the noisy casino floor Milo asked about Charlie's payment. "Like I told you, they gave me a hundred-grand and I haven't touched it." "Charlie, how did you receive the money? Was it a check or a wire transfer?"

The nervous F & B manager looked around, "I didn't see the payment. It just ended up in my bank account, just like my hotel paycheck." Milo asked if he could find the bank statement that showed the transfer. "We're leaving tomorrow or the next day. If you have the paperwork, leave it at the front desk for us." Charlie said he knew where his wife kept their banking statements. "I'll find it." Jordan smiled and said, "Thank you. That information might give us a lead to find out who's running this operation." She asked him to buy a disposable phone and call them if he needed them. "That way we can talk on a line we know is clean."

They watched as Charlie headed to the buffet to check the operation. Milo and Jordan went the other way stopping by the Keno lounge for a few games before their pizza dinner. "Do you think we can solve all this? It's pretty involved." Milo looked around the casino floor and escorted his "wife" to the roulette wheel. "We'll play one roll and if we win, the answer is yes we will solve this case." James placed a ten-dollar bill on the table. "Ten on seventeen please."

Jordan held her "hubby's" arm as the Croupier spun the wheel and dropped the ball. He proclaimed, "No more bets." Milo smiled and kissed his lady on the cheek. The wheel slowed, and the ball began to bounce around. Milo kissed her on the cheek again as they heard, "Seventeen black, odd". Jordan smiled as the Croupier put a marker on the winning number. He cleared the table layout and began to count out $350 in chips for Milo who tipped the Croupier as Jordan said, "Looks like we're going to solve this case."

Dinner with the Forbes' was fun. They joked and acted like everything was perfectly normal in their world. Milo told them, "We asked Charlie to give us his bank records. We might be able to trace the funds. If so, we could find out who's behind this." Jordan smiled and told them about their roulette win. "That means we're going to solve this case." Their waitress brought the check and Milo pulled out his cell phone. He clicked the scanner app and it flashed as the lady walked away. He showed the cell to everyone at the table. "It's happening everywhere." Milo was quiet for a moment and looked around the table as he said, "How about telling all the employees who are involved that they need to find another job?" Kate quickly said, "No, that's not our style." Jordan smiled and said, "I'm glad to hear that."

James finished his Scotch & Soda and looked at Jordan and Milo. "We operate a very fair and understanding business. I think we should have a one-on-one talk with each of the employees who are involved." He looked at Kate and said, "I think we'll tell them that the scanners are being eliminated and if anybody reacts adversely to the concept, those are the people we ask to leave." Kate nodded in agreement, "That's fair." James looked at Milo. "So, it's all up to you now. Try to find out who's behind this as soon as possible."

Milo told them, "As soon as I have Charlie's banking information, I'll need to use a secure computer. I might be able to figure out where the main operation is located." James said he would have Carl waiting in their surveillance center. "We have secure computers in there." Kate leaned over to quietly ask Jordan what they were going to do for the rest of the evening. Ms. Sutton smiled and told Kate, "We're gonna play Keno for a while and then head upstairs to play the 'act like we're newlyweds' game." Kate raised her eyebrows and whispered to Jordan that she and James play that game all the time. Milo looked over at the ladies who were talking quietly. "What are you two planning?" Jordan responded, "Nothing, just some girl-talk."

As they parted company James said, "Thank you for everything you've been able to accomplish so far." Milo told Mr. and Mrs. Forbes that they really enjoyed their time at the hotel. Jordan agreed. "Maybe we can return sometime and have a real vacation." Kate told them anytime they wanted to return, to just let them know. James moved close to Milo. "You'll probably be back if you're able to bring our problem to a close."

Milo shook hands with their new friends. "Yes, we'll return, and help you put an end to this mess." Kate hugged Jordan and Milo and thanked them for their help so far. "We'll see you both tomorrow." As Milo and Jordan walked arm-in-arm into the massive casino, Milo asked, "What do you want to do?" She opened her clutch bag and removed her Keno tickets. "I've got fifty games to check." Milo guided her toward the lounge. "Good, because I have some free drinking to do." When they entered the lounge, the Keno operator recognized Milo. "Mr. Lucky, welcome back. Are you playing?" He nodded yes, picked up a blank slip and marked his numbers while Jordan checked her fifty games. The Keno lady smiled at Jordan as she counted out her money, "You won seventy-five-dollars." Milo put his ticket on the counter, snagged five bucks from her winnings and put it on his ticket. The Keno operator said, "Five dollars, six numbers, one game." She handed him his ticket and wished him luck.

Jordan asked, "What are you playing?" He showed her the slip. "Six numbers again, good luck." They sat and ordered a free drink. Jordan leaned over to her guy. "I hope we can help James and Kate." Milo leaned in and kissed her lightly on her ruby lips. "I've been kicking around a few ideas. I think we can." The air blower started, and the Keno balls began to swirl around in the large cage. Their drinks arrived as they watched the Keno board. Jordan wasn't doing well.

"You would think this would be an easy game to win. There are 80 numbers, on the play sheet, they select 20 numbers each game and you would think you'd have a good chance." Milo was watching the balls and not really paying attention. Jordan continued, "I mean, I pick number 12 and number 11 or number 13 comes up. It's driving me nuts." The Keno caller said, "The final number is, 28."

Milo asked, "How did you do?" Jordan crumbled her sheet. "Nothing! What about you?" He started toward the counter, "I got 5 out of 6." He put his ticket on the counter. The Keno lady ran the sheet and said, "You won two-hundred-fifty-dollars. Congratulations." She counted out the money twice and Milo gave her a twenty-dollar tip. "Thank you." He put his winnings in his pocket and turned to Jordan.

"Well, what did you win?" He didn't answer; he just smiled. "Did you win a lot again?" He didn't talk, he just kept walking across the casino. "You aren't going to tell me? Where are we going?" Milo shrugged his shoulder and kept walking toward the fancy shops on Rodeo Drive North. RDN was bustling today. He opened the door of RDN Diamonds. Jordan smiled as she entered. "Why are we here?" Milo walked to the counter and talked to the smiling young lady who asked, "May I help you?" Milo said, "I would like to buy a ring." Jordan hugged him and kissed him on the cheek. He smiled at the sales lady. "Oh, she's my wife. This ring is for my girlfriend." Jordan, hit him on the arm. "I'm gonna get you for that." Milo looked at the confused sales girl. "I'm kidding. The ring is for my girlfriend who also happens to be my wife."

The young lady thought that was so sweet. She asked Jordan what she was looking for. Jordan had no idea. Milo saw a very comfortable-looking chair and decided this was the best place to be because Jordan could take a long time to make up her mind. And she did. For the next half-hour, she kept trying on rings and then walking to Milo to ask, "How do you like this one?" He kept saying the same thing, "That's nice dear, but it's up to you." Finally, after just forty-five minutes, P.I. Sutton made a decision, and it was a beautiful selection. The clerk rang up the sale and handed the sales order to Milo. How will you be paying? Milo said, "Cash." He opened the envelope with his Keno and Roulette winnings and counted out the money. The sales clerk finished the sale and told Jordan that her ring would be sized and ready for her in the morning. Jordan took the claim check and said she'd be back tomorrow. The sales clerk thanked them for shopping on RDN.

They walked slowly down Rodeo Drive North and Jordan was grinning from ear-to-ear. "I want to thank you for using your winnings to buy me a gift." Milo kept walking and talking, "Well, this has been a special time for me and I wanted you to have something from me to remind you of our escapade." Jordan hugged him around the waist. "Let's go upstairs and have a nice night unless you're too tired." Milo looked at his make-believe wife, "Me? Tired, I don't think so. Let's go."

CHAPTER 17

Breaking the Law

Milo opened his eyes and realized he lied last night when he said he wasn't tired. He was exhausted! Sliding out of the super-soft king size bed, he realized that Jordan's over-affectionate nightly displays were killing him. But he knew if he ever mentioned that, he'd never live it down. So, he quietly made his way to the shower with the multi-heads and used the warm water to bring himself back to life. He shaved and as he left the bathroom, he once again felt normal. "Time for coffee," he mumbled while crossing to the living room area of the suite. As he fixed a pot, the flashing message light on the house phone caught his eye.

He picked up the receiver, pressed the message button and found out that he had a delivery at the front desk. Milo finished making his coffee and called James to tell him that he thought the banking information from Charlie was waiting at the front desk. James said, "I'll alert Carl. He should be around all day, so if you get something, drop by anytime." Milo tickled Jordan's toes and gave her an update. She rolled over and peeked at Milo from under the sheet. "Good morning. I hope you enjoyed last night." Milo smiled and knew that he had to say yes, or be forever labeled an "old guy." "It was fantastic."

"We have to pick up something at the front desk and then meet up with Carl, so we can use his computer." Jordan held out her hand and said, "And we have to pick up my ring." She entered the bathroom and Milo knew what was coming—karaoke time without the music track. Milo thought this would be a good time to call Carol. "Good morning. Just wanted to tell you that we'll probably be home tomorrow or the next day." Carol said there were two stories about them in the newspaper. "I've got copies for both of you. The stories have caused the phones to ring constantly. You both have very long call lists." Milo assured her that this case would be over soon. Carol wanted to make sure they weren't in any trouble. Milo assured her they were fine. "See you tomorrow or the day after."

Jordan was dressed so quickly that Milo had to ask, "What happened to my partner?" Jordan looked confused. "I'm asking because my partner, Jordan Sutton is slow. She's super slow—slower than molasses in December." She glared at him, picked up her purse and said, "Get up and let's get some breakfast. We have work to do." Milo didn't know what to make of her orders. Then it hit him. She's excited about picking up her ring. He smiled, locked their door and put the Maid Service hanger on the handle.

Their first stop was the breakfast buffet. As soon as they were seated, Milo excused himself. "Go ahead and start eating, I'm going to the front desk to get our delivery." Jordan wasted no time. She got in line and decided to order a custom-made omelet with ten ingredients. Milo zigzagged through the gamblers as he made his way to the front desk. There were lots of people on the machines and small crowds at several of the table games. He waved at the Keno operators as he crossed to the front desk. The concierge saw him and immediately retrieved the envelope. "Good morning Mr. Starr. Here's your delivery. When will you be leaving us?" Milo thanked her for the envelope and said, "I think we'll be heading home tomorrow or the next day." She hoped they had enjoyed their stay. "Yes, it's been wonderful. We'll be back soon."

He joined Jordan who was about to start devouring her omelet. "What did you get?" Milo opened the stuffed envelope. "It's the banking stuff from Charlie." He started to read over the statements. "Are you going to eat?" He put the papers away and headed to the buffet. He was back before Jordan had taken two bites of her omelet. "That's all you're eating? Just a muffin and coffee?" Milo replied, "I'm not really that hungry. We'll have a big lunch and a bigger dinner." He opened the banking info again and began to make some notes in the margin. He called James to tell him that they would be heading to the I.T. Department in a few minutes. James said he already called Carl. "He'll be waiting for you." Milo took a bite of his English muffin and smiled at Jordan who said, "What?" Milo stopped looking at her. "I was just thinking about this trip and last night. I want you to know how much I've enjoyed being here with you." Jordan was happy to hear that news as she finished her breakfast and thanked him for the kind words. "I think it's better to play the part of a married couple than to actually be one." They both had a chuckle at that notion. "Are we going to see Carl now?" Milo said, "Yes, as soon as you're finished eating." She put her knife and fork down, handed him the receipt for breakfast and said, "Let's go."

Carl met them and asked Milo, "What do you need to do?" "I need to tap into my ultra-secure computer system in L.A. and use it to mask this I.P. address so I can do what I need to do in private." Carl stood and offered his chair, "Okay, you can use my computer. It's not on the hotel's system. Should I leave you alone?" Milo said, "Yes, because we're going to be breaking the law. You shouldn't be here for that." Carl smiled and then realized that Milo wasn't kidding. "I'll be back in a while."

When they were alone, the first thing Milo did was scan the office for listening devices. It was clean. Jordan pulled up a chair and watched as Milo connected to his very secure home/office system. He hid the I.P. address behind several online firewalls and asked Jordan to read the bank routing number of the transactions he marked. Jordan looked over Charlie's data. "This is a strange number." Milo explained that was a secure account number in the Cayman Islands. She read the number slowly and then checked it again to make sure she read it correctly. It didn't take Milo very long to link into Charlie's bank account and then access the off-shore Cayman account where the hundred-thousand-dollar deposit originated. He told Jordan to see if the printer was on. She looked, "It is." As soon as Milo had all the information on the screen, he sent it to the printer and quickly got out of the account.

He looked over the printout and thought he might

have the origin of the payment to Charlie. Milo checked to make sure his I.P. address was still masked. It was, so he asked Jordan to read the routing number at the bottom of the page. He typed as she read and then he asked her to re-read the number. "I don't want to make any mistakes." He watched as his masked system connected with a bank in West Los Angeles, California. He hit the print button and immediately ended the session. Jordan picked up the printout as Carl stepped in to ask if they were finished. "Yes, we are. Thank you." Carl asked if they could tell him what they were doing. Milo said, "I'm not really sure, yet." Carl wondered if the hotel would be pulling the plug on all the over-charging. "Eventually, but not right now. Things are going to stay as they are until we figure out who's running this operation." Carl said he understood and wouldn't say anything to anybody. Jordan told him, "That's the best plan, for now."

Once in the casino they called James and asked if they could head back to L.A. tomorrow. "I think we might have a lead on the company that's behind all of this." James thought that was good news and mentioned that he and Kate would fly back with them tomorrow afternoon. "It's time we got back to work too." Milo said, "I'll get Jordan to start packing early." James asked if they would like to join them for dinner that evening. Milo accepted the invite and told Jordan about their plans. "We're dining with James and Kate tonight and we're flying back with them tomorrow afternoon. So, let's go and get packed." Jordan raised her voice, "Are you kidding? Not until I pick up my ring." Milo took her arm, "Okay, RDN Diamonds first, then we pack."

CHAPTER 18

Back to L.A.

Jordan was up early, packing. "Come on, sleepy-head, time to get up." Milo sat up in bed to ask, "What are you doing and why are you doing it so early?" She was wide-awake and folding a blouse. "We're being picked up at three and we're flying home about four, I just wanted to be ready early." Milo looked at the digital clock, "But it's only…never mind. I'll get up and get moving. I'm all packed by the way." He called the Food and Beverage Department and left a message for Charlie, *"Charlie, I picked up the envelope, we'll talk soon."*

Jordan finished packing and left her bags in the living room area of the suite. During their breakfast, Milo couldn't resist saying how much he enjoyed watching his lovely partner showing off her new ring at dinner. She smiled, "You can't get mad at that, I'm happy with my gift." Milo replied, "I'm not mad, it was just cute. Did we do everything we needed to do here?" Jordan opened her phone and looked at her original list. "Everything is checked off except the cigar store and the hat shop." Milo wondered if they had to go there. She didn't think so. "If there are people using the scanners there, Charlie will know who they are." Milo agreed, "You're right and if James and Kate interview all the people involved, everything will end eventually."

Milo called the front desk to tell them about their bags and departure time. He thanked the concierge for her help during their stay and said they would be in the Keno lounge in the afternoon waiting for their driver. Once they reached the casino level they were hungry and ready for some slot action. Jordan played a few pulls on their way to breakfast and won a dollar. She cashed out and showed him her one-dollar voucher. "I'll keep this for our next trip, or frame it as a souvenir."

Breakfast was fantastic as was all the food they had on the trip. "We have to tell James and Kate how much we enjoyed the restaurants." Jordan made a mental note. After they stuffed themselves, they decided to stay in the casino and try a few of the new slot machines. Milo couldn't believe how elaborate the slots had become. He leaned over to Jordan, "The machine sings to me as it takes my money. I'm going to the Keno lounge." He began playing a few games, while looking at his email. He called Carol and got her voice mail. "We'll be back in the office on Monday." Jordan found him and asked how he was doing? "I've only won two-dollars today."

They waved at Charlie who was crossing the casino. He made a quick detour to join them. "Hey Charlie, we're leaving today." Charlie thanked them for helping the hotel. "Do we keep everything as-is?" Milo told him, "Yes, for now. The information you provided was a big help. Once we wrap everything up, Mr.

Forbes will tell you how he wants to proceed." Charlie thanked them again for coming to help. "I hope we end all of this quickly." Jordan assured him they would be working on it. Milo got a call from the concierge telling him that their limo had arrived. "Charlie, we're outta here. We'll talk to you soon."

During the flight back to Los Angeles, James and Kate let Milo and Jordan know how happy they were with their work during their ten days at the hotel. "We really can't thank you enough." Kate asked if they had a good time. Jordan said, "It was busy, but very enjoyable. You spoiled us, for sure." Milo added, "We're not finished you know. This was only the beginning. We have to figure out who's behind all of this, and get everything stopped." Jordan opened her purse and handed Kate the remaining cash they received when they started. "No, put that back. That's yours. Don't forget to send us an invoice for your work." Jordan smiled and thanked her.

James wanted to know how he could assist with the case. Milo wondered if he thought Charlie knew the Food and Beverage Managers at other hotels. "He probably does." "Do you know the owners of other hotels around town?" James said he knew almost all of them. "We have an association. Should I call them?" Milo told him not to call anybody right now. "We really don't know who's involved yet. Once we do, then you can call everybody."

Jordan told them that they would be in touch as soon as all the pieces of the puzzle came together. We'll keep you posted on everything." Kate said she would alert their secretary, Della. "I'll tell her to put your calls through to one of us." Milo asked, "Tomorrow is

Sunday, right?" James replied, "Yes, it is." Jordan added, "I wasn't sure either. We were so busy doing things on the list and with no clocks around, we lost track of time and even days. I want to thank you for the necklace and for the use of the wedding rings."

Jordan held out her hand and admired the beautiful ring again and then told Milo to hand his over. He smiled as he removed the ring and said, "Yes, it's time for the 'divorce'. Thank you for everything." Jordan put the ring Milo bought her on her right hand. Kate asked if they were winners while they were at the hotel. "Yes, Milo won at Keno, that's how he paid for my ring and you folks bought me that beautiful necklace. Yes, we were really big winners. Thank you". Milo joked, "I didn't get a ring and a necklace." Jordan swatted him with her purse. James and Kate were happy that Sutton and Starr had fun and won something.

They were met at the airport by Marcus and his shiny Limo. Jordan started to shake hands with Kate who ignored Jordan's hand and embraced her and Milo instead. James was also a hugger. He opened the limo door as Marcus put their luggage in the trunk. "Thanks for everything. We'll talk soon." The limo door closed, and they rolled off toward the condo. Marcus asked, "Did you enjoy your trip?" "Yes, we had a great time. The Forbes' are wonderful people."

Once they got home Milo called Carol to tell her they would be in about noon on Monday. Carol said she would see them then. "I want a complete report of your ten-day stakeout." Milo ended the call. "Carol wants a complete report on our stakeout. I'm going to leave the storytelling up to you. She always knows when I'm lying."

CHAPTER 19

Breaking the Law Again

Jordan opened the sliding door to the lanai and several windows to air out the condo. She held up her hand and flashed her new bauble. "Thank you for the ring. Did we bring home anything for Carol?" Milo, who was sitting on the couch just staring into space said, "No. We couldn't without telling her what we were doing. Now, until we wrap up this case, we can't say anything about it. You better have a good story ready." Jordan was thinking out loud, "Let's get her some candy and a gift certificate to one of her favorite stores." She headed for the bedroom to unpack. Milo was still trying to figure out how to proceed with the case when Jordan asked, "Would you like a beer?" He mumbled a faint yes as he turned on his computer system.

Moments later Jordan arrived with the cold brew. Milo took his first swig and pressed the cold glass bottle to his forehead. "I'm going to break the law again tonight." Jordan smiled and ran her hands up the back of his neck. "I can hardly wait." Milo took a second sip, "No, not that kind of lawbreaking. I'm going to be doing some heavy-duty hacking." Jordan settled back on the couch to watch the show.

"How did you learn to do all that?" Milo told her all about one of his early exploits as he went online. He was taking some advanced computer classes in college that involved a few very difficult tests. "One took the class over six hours to complete. Some students didn't make it, they left early. They just couldn't do it." She smiled at him. "But you finished?" Milo raised his beer to her. "Yes, I did. It was sort of a scavenger hunt on the computer. I had to break into several websites and servers all over the world. We had to print out proof we'd been there and do it all without being detected. I didn't get caught and received an A." Milo's machine beeped. He was now on-line connected to a remote server in Ireland that could only be reached after 25 other servers lined up to repeat his signal. He tried to explain what was going on, but Jordan didn't really get it.

He turned on his printer and opened the banking information they received from Charlie. They checked deposits in the Las Vegas bank against withdrawals from an off-shore account owned by a shell corporation with a mailing address in Dubai. He stopped for a moment and Jordan asked, "Did you hit a dead end?" Milo began to type again. "No, just a small wall that I was able to pass through." The screen displayed a lot of banking records which Milo printed quickly and then he moved on. He was having trouble back-tracking the deposits to the off-shore account since they were emanating from many different banks. Milo pointed to the screen. "Look, they're piggybacking the deposits from one bank to another. It's a good way to hide what they're doing, but not quite good enough." He hit the print button again and disengaged his connection.

"Not bad, huh?" Jordan had no idea what he was doing or talking about. He picked up the printouts. "I just hacked some of the world's most unhackable banks and I did it in less than five minutes." Jordan seemed awestruck, "Wow that's great! So, you know who's involved?" Milo laughed at his lovely partner. "I don't have a clue who's doing anything yet, but I do know *what* they are doing or rather did." Milo said he had to get into some records from a bank here in town. "I think the people behind this are right here in the Los Angeles area." Jordan was shocked, "Not in Las Vegas?" Milo picked up his printouts and just did a simple web search for the bank routing numbers. His computer beeped. "I was right, the transactions all started from a bank in downtown L.A." They both sat quietly. Jordan took his empty bottle to the kitchen. "Now what?" Milo looked at the clock on his computer. "It's not too late, I think I'll call James and give him an update."

James picked up on the first ring, and was shocked that Milo was already working on the case. "The payments started here in Los Angeles. Later tonight, I'm going to attempt to learn more about the owners of the accounts. I'll keep you posted. Jordan and I want to thank you again for your hospitality at the hotel." James thanked them for their help so far and was looking forward to their next report. "Be sure to send us an invoice for your work so far."

Jordan was shower-singing, so Milo attempted to learn more about the local accounts involved in these crimes. He kept getting the same answer. "Z Account and Z Corp. Account." He scribbled those names on one of the printouts and made a note to ask James if that meant anything to him. Jordan came out of the shower wearing one of her super short robes. "Make any progress?" He looked at his lady and noted she was still wearing her new ring. "It needed a shower too. What did you find out?"

Milo replied, "All I found out is the accounts are all called Z something." Jordan scrunched her face, "What the hell does that mean?" Milo had no idea. "I'm going to ask James if he knows." Jordan asked about their next move. Milo stood and walked to their lanai. He took a deep breath of L.A. air and headed to his bar. "My next move is opening another beer. Want one?" Jordan declined. Milo took his drink to the lanai. "I have a couple of ideas to run by you." He sat in one of their comfy chairs and motioned for Jordan to sit.

"How about this? What if we tell Charlie to pull all the scanners? He can tell the employees that they are switching over to a new system. What do you think will happen?" Jordan sort of went into cop-mode. "I think a massive shutdown like that will piss off the people who are running this thing." Milo sort of agreed, "Alright, let's say they're really pissed, what will they do?" Jordan grabbed his beer and took a sip. "Well, Leroy, the food and beverage guy who had the job before Charlie wanted to stop this operation and somebody killed him. So?" Milo said, "So, you're thinking that if we stop this cold, someone could end up like Leroy." Jordan kept his beer. "That's what I'm thinking."

Milo sat thinking for a moment. "Since credit card fraud is both a state and federal crime. I think we should call our good friend and FBI super-star, CR Reid. I believe we could use his help on this. What do you think?" She handed him his almost empty beer. "I think you're right. Call him. You'll probably get his voice mail, but give it a shot." Milo did as he was told, and did get his voice mail. "Hi CR, Milo here. Jordan and I are working on a case that *you're* gonna want to get involved in. Call us ASAP!" Milo raised his empty beer bottle to his lovely partner. "He'll call us because he knows we're publicity hounds and he would love a raise."

Jordan smiled and asked, "Shall we power down for the night?" Milo put his empty bottle on the bar, "Yes, ex-wife, I'm ready for bed and a real vacation." She stopped, "Yes, you're right. But I did enjoy being fake-married to you." Milo kissed her and whispered, "Me too."

CHAPTER 20

Back at Work

Jordan, carrying a cute gift bag, entered the office and greeted Carol who was very happy to see them. "Boy, am I glad you're back! I've been going crazy sitting around the house." Carol hugged Jordan and Milo too. "I even missed you, boss." Milo thanked her for the backhanded compliment as Carol followed him into his office. "So, tell me all about the stakeout." Milo turned on his computer and printer. "Ask Jordan, she kept notes on everything we did." Carol handed him a three-page printout. "Here's your call list. It's going to take you several weeks to get it all done." Milo thanked Carol, who left in search of Jordan and the story of their stakeout.

Milo sat in his very soft chair and began to look over the call sheets. Carol listed the calls by category, interviews, robberies, missing persons, insurance fraud and two calls from CR. Milo was trying to figure out where to start when Carol buzzed him, "You have a call on line one." "Hi, this is Milo." It was CR Reid who wanted to know what his late-night message meant. "Hello, FBI super-star, we need to talk to you in person, when can you come over?" CR said he'd be free about three o'clock. "I'm only coming if Jordan will be there too. You're okay, but Jordan is *really* okay." Milo assured him that his partner would be there. "See you at three."

Milo popped into Jordan's nicely scented office. "CR is coming over today at three. He said he would only show up if you're here." She fluffed her hair. "I have that kind of effect on law enforcement officers." Milo headed back to his office laughing. "You are so full of beans." As he passed Carol's desk, she said, "Thank you for the candy and very extravagant gift card." Milo glanced at Carol displaying the gifts. "You deserve it. Spend it all and get something pretty for yourself." Milo decided to buckle down and start to return the calls on his list. But first, he checked with Carol and Jordan to see if they had any appointments scheduled. They didn't, so he told them he'd start the master list. He opened their new sliding wall partition and began writing their schedule on the hidden whiteboard.

Milo set up two magazine interviews and arranged a meeting with an insurance company regarding a fraud claim. He put the three appointments on the whiteboard and decided to stop calling potential clients until they talked to their FBI friend, CR. He was worried that the credit card case could get more involved. Jordan said she wasn't having any luck. "Nobody is around. I've been leaving messages all over town." She looked at the schedule Milo started on the whiteboard. "Wow, you were able to set up meetings? You must have had all the good phone numbers."

It was five minutes past three when CR entered the reception area. "Hi Carol. This place looks amazing. You and Jordan must have spruced everything up. I know it wasn't done by you know who." Carol laughed and agreed. "You're right, we did it all." She opened Milo's door, "Your three o'clock appointment is here." Milo looked up and smiled, "Sorry but he's five minutes, no make that seven minutes late."

CR thanked Carol and entered Milo's office. "Wow, I like what the girls did with this place. It was time you classed up your act." Milo welcomed their old friend and buzzed Jordan, "Ms. Sutton our three o'clock appointment is finally here." Milo was about to ask if CR wanted coffee when Carol and Jordan entered. Carol put a tray with a coffee service on Milo's desk and Jordan hugged CR. "It's good to see you. When's the wedding?" CR told them that his bride-to-be hadn't picked a date, yet. Milo poured coffee for everyone and asked, "What's she waiting for? Is she trying to decide if you're really the one?"

CR took his coffee and stared at Jordan and Milo. "When are you two getting hitched?" Jordan glared at him and said, "That's never gonna happen! I've been down that road and once was enough." CR took the hint and changed the subject, "What did you want to talk to me about?" Milo pushed several keys on his computer and the wide-blade shutters slowly closed three interior lights popped on and his door locked. "We can talk now." CR looked around Milo's swank office. "Is this place a secure environment?" Milo replied, "It is. We got the work done after our last case." Jordan added, "We thought it was time for some high-end security."

Milo handed CR a brochure for the Golden Oasis Hotel. "This is the case we're working on." He and Jordan went on to explain that the owners of the hotel called them because of the publicity they received from solving several high-profile cases. They told their longtime friend about the credit card fraud, the murder of the original beverage manager, the electronic bugs in the office and the threat that Charlie Brady had received.

CR asked how long Mr. Brady had been involved in this. They explained that he was promoted when their original beverage manager was killed. "They told Brady to keep everything running as is or he'd end up like his predecessor. They paid him to make sure the overcharging continued." Jordan added, "He received a hundred grand, but he never spent a dime of the money. It's in his bank." Milo told CR, "We used that deposit to trace the money flow. So far, I've tracked the payment from a Cayman Islands account and the owner might be here in Southern California."

CR had a lot of who, what, where, when and why questions and was shocked that Sutton & Starr had an answer for everything. "So, what's your next move and what am I doing here?" Milo asked if CR thought this idea might work. "We all go to Las Vegas and you arrest Charlie Brady in his bugged office. That way, the people who are running this operation know about the arrest. Then we pull the plug on all of the portable scanners."

Jordan said, "We then have the hotel's owners, James and Kate Forbes, interview each of the employees who use the scanners. We want to find out how much these employees are making per month on this scam, then tell them it's over and see what happens. Milo asked CR, "What do you think of that idea?" Their old college chum thought for a moment and then offered this, "Well, I think that will work, but I also think it will really upset whoever is running this scam. How do you plan to find the people in charge?" Milo looked at their friend and said, "Remember what we did on the mutilation murders?" He didn't see a big reaction from CR.

"We found all the people involved, because you arrested them and that's what caused the people behind the killings to show their faces." CR finished his coffee and looked at Jordan. "How long have I known you two?" Jordan was about to answer when CR cut her off. "Since college, right? In all that time, you've had some whacky ideas and no matter how crazy they sounded, I always listened." He looked at each of them. "Well, I'm listening again. I think this plan is just crazy enough to work. Plus, I get a trip to Las Vegas out of it."

Milo and Jordan smiled, and she said, "I'm glad you like the idea. I think we should see the hotel owners and tell them what we're planning." CR said, "Where do they live?" She told him about their accounting business in Beverly Hills and said she would set up a meeting as quickly as possible. Milo said, "This operation is costing them a lot of money in refunds for the over-charging, so the faster we work, the better it will be for them."

Jordan picked up the phone to call Forbes and Associates. She was put right through to James. She told him they would like to come over to talk to him in person. He said his schedule was clear all afternoon. Jordan asked CR, "Can you go with us now?" CR nodded yes. Jordan continued her conversation. "We'll be bringing CR Reid from the FBI with us. We'll be over in about an hour."

They told Carol they would be out for a while. "If you're going to lunch, bring me something." Milo said, "We're not going to lunch, but I will bring you something on our way back." Carol waved as the phone rang. "Sutton and Starr Private Investigators, how may I help you?" She listened, "Yes he's right here." She handed the phone to Milo. "This is Milo Starr." He listened for a moment, made a few uh-huh responses and then the phone went dead. Milo turned and smiled. "Just a junk call. We'll be back in a little while." The trio headed for the elevator and as the doors closed Milo said, "That wasn't a junk call. It was some guy telling us to stay out of their business in Vegas, if we know what's good for us."

As the elevator doors opened CR started to cough and laugh. "That guy doesn't know you very well because you have never stayed out of anything and neither of you knows what's good for you." They were all laughing as they piled into Milo's car and headed for Beverly Hills.

CHAPTER 21

Forbes & Associates

"Where are you taking me? You said we were going to meet some accountants. This place looks like one of our old college buildings." Milo told CR to relax, "We're not going back to school. This is their office building." As they left the car, CR looked around at the mansion-like building sitting well back from the street, and seemed very impressed. "I wish our FBI office looked like this." Jordan laughed, "We like it too, but we probably couldn't even afford the gardener's fee." Before Milo could press the doorbell, a voice said, "Welcome Mr. Starr." The massive door's auto-lock was disengaged, and Milo opened it for Jordan and CR.

Della, the Forbes' secretary, welcomed them and asked if they would like a beverage. Jordan replied, "Thank you, but not right now." Della escorted them to the main office where they were greeted by James Forbes. Milo introduced CR who handed his FBI business card to James. "Welcome, please sit. Della, would you have Kate join us." CR was taking in the opulence of the building, the office and the general demeanor of their host. CR could tell Mr. Forbes was a well-educated gentleman who came from "old money." Milo set his cell phone app to BLOCK SIGNALS.

It didn't take long for Kate to appear. Now CR was doubly impressed. In his mind, Mrs. Forbes could have been a top runway model. She greeted everyone. Milo introduced their long-time friend, CR. "Welcome, would you like coffee?" Milo nodded yes and said, "Only if it's your private blend." Kate smiled and buzzed Della, "Would you bring coffee for everyone, please?" Milo smiled and told CR that he was going to love the coffee. James said he remembered CR from one of the press conferences and wanted to know why they brought him in to help.

Milo told James and Kate that he had tracked the money trail from several off-shore accounts, but every account was just labeled Z Account or Z Corp Account. "Does either of those names mean anything to you?" Kate and James both indicated no, and Milo continued. "We brought CR up to speed on everything and we've come up with a possible solution." Kate asked CR what he thought he could do for them. The FBI agent told them that he had known Milo and Jordan since college, and at times, they had some very unusual ways of solving crimes. "That's why I listened to them when they told me about your problem. I think they have a plan to bring everything to a conclusion."

Milo motioned to Jordan and she began. "Kate, I know you had talked about raising the salary of those involved to compensate for the money they would be losing, but we don't think that's the answer. Each of them is guilty of these crimes." Milo helped her out. "But, we also know that some of them, maybe all of them, didn't have a choice. CR, many of the employees were threatened to keep overcharging customers. So, here's what we have in mind. We all go back to the hotel and start to dismantle everything." Della knocked at the door and delivered the coffee service. "Thank you, Della."

Kate handed each of them a cup and saucer as she asked, "All right, we all fly back to the hotel and what do we do first?" CR took a sip of coffee and said, "Milo told us that the Food and Beverage Manager, ah…" James stepped in, "Charlie Brady." CR continued, "Yes, Charlie, thank you. His office is bugged so if we arrest him in his office, the people behind this will hear what's going on and know that the operation is being discontinued." Milo added, "But we don't really arrest him." James and Kate looked puzzled. Jordan continued. "We only have CR pretend to arrest Charlie. We then take him and his family to an undisclosed location for their protection." James liked the plan so far, "What do Kate and I do?" Milo laid out the rest of their idea. "We ask Charlie for a list of every employee who is involved and instead of talking to them privately, as you mentioned before, we bring them all together and tell them that the scanners are being phased out. You'll need to speak privately to anyone who is opposed to the new system."

Jordan looked at James and Kate, "We know you want to be fair with everybody, but if someone objects, they have to be dealt with on an individual basis." James wondered if there would be any repercussions because of the way this was being handled. CR said, "With me and my FBI badge in the room while you talk to them, I think those involved will realize that this is very serious. The fact that they can keep their jobs, with no charges filed against them, is a big plus." Kate asked if any of them would be in danger. Milo said he didn't think so, since they were talking about a quick resolution to everything. "Remember, nobody knows who's using the scanners except Charlie." CR added, "If this becomes a federal case, then my guys would be involved. Otherwise, it's an in-house problem that you should handle."

They all decided to fly to Las Vegas early Thursday. James said he would contact Charlie and have him set up the meeting with everyone who's involved. "We'll have Della confirm your rooms for the weekend." Kate told them that they would have the limo pick them up Thursday morning at nine. "Will that work for you?" Jordan replied, "That will be great if I can get Milo up and moving that early." Kate hugged Sutton and Starr and shook hands with CR. "We'll see all of you on Thursday." Milo said, "Let's hope we can put an end to all of this." As they were leaving the beautiful office building, James said, "You didn't send us an invoice for your ten days at the hotel. Have your people send that over." Milo said he would.

Once outside CR was grinning as he said, "You have people?" Milo remotely unlocked the car and CR kept needling him, "Come on, you gonna tell me where you got people?" Milo opened the driver's side door, "Shut up and get in the car. We have people. You just don't know them." CR slammed his door, laughed and said, "Neither do you." Jordan told CR to be at their condo by eight-thirty on Thursday. "You can ride to the airport with us." Milo smirked, "In a limo, driven by one of our people."

CHAPTER 22

Off to Vegas Tomorrow

As they parked at the office Jordan hoped they wouldn't be there too long, "I still have a few things to pack." Milo assured her that since they had no appointments he only wanted to finish up a few things before they left for Vegas. Milo went directly into his office and prepared the invoice for James and Kate. He asked Jordan to review the invoice before they sent it. She glanced at it but felt strange about charging them. "They gave us so much." She said everything looked in order, so Milo handed Carol a printout of the invoice and asked her to send it to Forbes and Associates. "It's for our ten-day stakeout. We're leaving tomorrow for four days and will be working for Forbes and Associates again."

Carol loved the idea, "So, we're closed Thursday until Monday?" Jordan said, "Yes, we're flying to Las Vegas to help them with a problem at their hotel." Carol was all smiles. Jordan questioned her, "I thought you go crazy at home." She smiled again, "Not this time, everybody is going to an amusement park for two days and I told them I was too tired to walk all over hell and back. So, I will be home alone! You guys have fun and remember, don't get married unless I'm invited." She went to work on the invoice. Jordan smiled as she entered Milo's office. "I told Carol about our weekend mission and she reminded us not to get married unless she was invited." Milo returned the smile just as Carol buzzed. *"How do you want this invoice sent?"* Milo told her email would be fine.

Milo was up early the next morning with a cup of coffee in his new favorite Golden Oasis Hotel mug when Jordan lumbered out of bed. She muttered something that sounded like, "I smell coffee." Milo looked at his partner and thought he already knew the answer to his question, but he asked anyway. "Are you packed?" Jordan filled her mug and finally noticed Milo. "Did you say something?" "I just asked if you were packed." Jordan trudged toward the bathroom, "Yes, my small case is by the door." Milo looked and couldn't believe his eyes. She *was* all packed.

CR was right on-time as was their driver, Marcus, who attended to their luggage. Jordan greeted him, "Thank you, Marcus. This is CR Reid, he's joining us for the weekend." Marcus acknowledged their guest and told them he knew there would be a third passenger. Within minutes they were off to the airport. Marcus lowered the glass partition and said, "Mr. and Mrs. Starr and Mr. Reid if you'd like some coffee, I filled three thermal mugs." Milo thanked him as he passed around the mugs. CR commented, "Mr. and Mrs.? What's that all about?" Jordan explained their fake marriage on their first trip to the hotel. "How long were you there?" Milo said, "Not very long, only ten days." Jordan added, "It was wonderful." CR wondered how he could get that kind of work. Milo raised his mug and smiled, "You can't, because you won't leave your cushy job."

They rolled up to the airport's inspection gate and Marcus lowered the rear window. The guard looked in and CR flashed his badge. The guard nodded, and the limo rolled slowly toward a private jet. CR saw James and Kate waiting for them and said, "Wow, we're going first-class today!" Milo got out of the limo and said, "Buddy, you ain't seen nothin' yet." Kate greeted everyone and within minutes they were on board. They buckled up as the flight service crew handed each of them a flute of champagne. James raised his glass. "We want to thank all of you for helping us. Milo, we received your invoice. Thank you." Milo looked at CR and said quietly, "They got our invoice." Milo grinned and raised his glass to CR and whispered, "My people sent that over."

As the aircraft taxied down the runway, James received a text. "Charlie, our Food and Beverage Manager contacted all the employees who are involved in the overcharging. He wants to know when we'd like to meet with them." Milo asked James to text Charlie. "Let's set that up for early Saturday morning, if possible." Jordan said, "If that works we might wrap up everything this weekend." During the flight, they discussed their plan, and everyone agreed that it was the correct approach. Milo thought for a moment and said, "Then I guess we're all set." Kate reached in her purse. "Not quite." She handed Jordan the two small purple bags. Jordan smiled and as she handed one bag to Milo, she said, "Milo Starr will you marry me?" He was shocked by the statement but understood when he saw the purple bag. He removed the plain gold wedding band from the bag. "Yes, Ms. Sutton, I'll marry you for four days." They both put the rings on their fingers as Kate said, "Now you're all set." Milo smiled, "Yes we are, Mrs. Starr." CR looked totally confused. Jordan smiled, "We'll explain everything later. Just don't ever mention this to Carol."

The concierge was front and center to greet Mr. and Mrs. Forbes and said, "Welcome back Mr. and Mrs. Starr, I see you're just in for the weekend." Jordan smiled and said, "Yes, a short trip this time." She also welcomed CR Reid, who still didn't understand the make-believe marriage. James let them know that Charlie was expecting them to drop by today to explain everything. They quickly checked in at the desk and Milo took his "wife" by the arm, "Let's see Charlie before we go to our rooms." They made their way through the bustling casino and found the Food and Beverage Manager working at his desk. They waved at him to join them. When they were back in the noisy casino James introduced CR, "And of course you remember Milo and Jordan." Charlie greeted everyone and escorted them to the small coffee shop off the lobby. He motioned to the waitress to bring coffee for six.

Milo set his phone app to BLOCK SIGNAL. James said they had a plan. "Milo and Jordan will tell you what we have in mind." Milo gave him the rundown. "You've already done the first part by compiling the list of all the scanner users. How many are there?" Charlie told them there are seventy-five using the skimmers. "I set a meeting with all of them for nine AM, Saturday morning." Milo thought for a moment, "That's great Charlie. We need to talk to the repair company tomorrow, so Saturday is the perfect time to talk with the employees." Milo continued, "I think once the scanners are all taken off-line, someone will call a repair crew to check the problem." CR added, "Then we arrest that crew." Charlie didn't fully understand. Jordan explained that on Friday they wanted to meet the repair company by causing a scanner outage.

Milo continued, "Charlie, at the employee meeting we'd like you to talk to them first. Introduce CR Reid from the FBI and tell them that all scanners will be taken off-line." Jordan told Charlie that at that point in the meeting, Mr. and Mrs. Forbes would address the group. James said, "We want them to know it's over and their reward is keeping their jobs." Kate added, "This mess has cost us a lot of money and we'll see if there are any dissenters."

Milo told him about the phony arrest in his bugged office and following that, you'll leave the hotel, meet up with your family and take a short vacation. He looked relieved, but was still a little confused. "So, I won't really be arrested?" Jordan assured him it was a ploy to get the people behind all of this to realize that it was over. The Food and Beverage Manager was very relieved and said he liked what he heard. He then looked at James and Kate. He shook their hands and thanked them for being such compassionate people.

Kate smiled at him and said, "Charlie, we know you're only involved because you were threatened." He told them, "They said I was to tell everybody who got involved that they couldn't just stop, they just had to keep doing it." Milo added, "So, everyone was being forced to do this?" Charlie said, "Yes, some didn't want to get involved and they just quit their job. A few are doing it now and hate it and others don't mind since they are making a little extra money. Let's see what happens at the meeting." Charlie asked if he should alert his family that they would be taking a quick trip. CR told him he should make the call on Jordan's phone. "Where are we going?" CR looked at James for the answer. James smiled and said, "You're going to Disneyland for a few days on us." Jordan handed Charlie her phone, "Call your family now and tell them about the trip. You'll be leaving Saturday after the meeting."

Charlie loved the idea and immediately called his wife who was excited to hear about the trip. He handed Jordan her phone with a big smile on his face. "My wife couldn't believe it and is thrilled. She said she wouldn't tell the kids until Saturday." Charlie started for his office with a big smile on his face. Milo stopped him by saying, "Remember, CR is going to arrest you on Saturday after the meeting so whoever is on the other side of those listening devices will think you've been arrested for real." Charlie understood as he headed to his office.

James and Kate thought that went well and invited their guests to dinner at the RDN steakhouse at seven.

CR said, "Thank you. I'll be there, I'm starving." Milo and Jordan thanked James and Kate. "See you at seven." They headed toward the elevators. CR said, "Tomorrow's going to be intense." Milo asked, "What floor?" CR said, "Ten. What about you?" Milo punched 10 and 22. "We're a little higher." As CR exited the elevator, Jordan said, "We'll see you at seven at the steakhouse. Good luck in the casino."

CHAPTER 23

Time for an Arrest

"Thanks for dragging me along last night. That was the best steak I've ever eaten." Milo and Jordan smiled and reminded CR that they ate like that every night at The Golden Oasis. "You were doing that for ten days?" Milo shrugged as if it were no big deal and said, "Of course. Wait till you try the buffet, it's sensational too." As they walked through the casino they passed the Keno lounge and Jordan commented, "We had a great time here too. Do you play Keno?" CR said he didn't really know how to play. Jordan took his arm, "We'll teach you and if you're lucky like my partner, you have to buy your fiancé a gift." Milo opened the door of the Dublin Pub and ushered Jordan and CR inside. They selected a table in the corner and waited for the bartender to approach them. "Welcome back, Mr. and Mrs." He paused, and Jordan said, "Starr." Tim nodded, "Yes, Mr. and Mrs. Starr, what kin I git fur ya?" Milo ordered three glasses of iced tea. Tim headed back to the bar as James, Kate and Charlie entered.

James and Kate shook hands all around and asked, "What are we doing here?" Milo smiled and told them they were having iced tea. "Would you like a glass?" Kate said, "Sure, but I know you didn't ask us here to drink tea." Milo set his scanner app to BLOCK SIGNAL. "It's time to pull the plug on Tim's scanner and see what happens. Let's see who shows up to fix the problem." Milo nodded to Charlie who approached the bar. "Tim we're going to use your scanner to trigger an outage. We want to see how long it takes for the repair company to respond. Do you have your unit here?" Tim removed the scanner from his arm and handed it to Charlie who disconnected the unit. "Let's see what happens." Tim put a tray with six glasses of iced tea on the bar. Charlie carefully carried the tray to the table.

He told everyone that Tim's scanner was off-line. "Now, we just wait for the repair company." He looked at CR. "Do you intend to arrest whoever comes?" CR said, "Probably not. But I do want to interrogate 'em." CR told James and Kate how much he loved the hotel and last night's dinner. Jordan said they were going to teach CR how to play Keno today. James added, "Milo won at Keno during their first stay." Jordan showed off the ring on her right hand. "He bought me this with his winnings." Milo quickly said, "It is *not* a wedding ring." Kate laughed, "No, it's a promise ring." They talked and laughed for about twenty minutes.

When an older gentleman carrying a small shoulder bag entered the pub, they stopped talking and watched him. Tim looked over at Charlie and nodded. The repair guy asked, "What's wrong with your system this time?" He opened his bag and put his small laptop on the bar. Charlie approached the repair guy and said, "Nothing's wrong." The man turned to Charlie. "Yeah, something's messed up. The system is not responding again."

Charlie read the repair man's name tag. "Bob, I want you to meet the person who turned off the system." CR stepped to the bar and displayed his FBI badge. "He did it." Bob was flustered. "But, you can't do that. My boss told me to get everything working or I'd lose my job." CR asked, "Who's your boss?" Bob looked very confused and stuttered as he said. "It's, it's George Cullen at CC repair." CR said, "We should speak with Mr. Cullen, for sure." Milo asked, "Bob, what do you do when you come here?"

The repairman opened his laptop and showed them what he does. "I log onto your system number two and see where the trouble is. Then I identify the problem and re-connect what's off-line." He pointed to the screen. "See? Here's the credit card scanner at this location. It's red and that means it's not working." Milo looked at the screen. "That's all you do?" Bob nodded, "No, I also look over the entire operation to see if there are any other outages." He searched and didn't see any other problems. "Everything else seems to be okay." Jordan had an idea. "Bob, can you call your boss and ask him to come over here? Maybe tell him you have a problem you can't solve." Bob looked at CR and asked if he was in trouble. CR told him no. "Looks like you're just doing your job. We'd still like to talk to your boss." Bob picked up his cell phone and called the office as Jordan had suggested. "Mr. Cullen will be here in about ten or fifteen minutes."

While they waited for the boss, Milo asked Bob how long it took to install a credit card system. "I don't know; I've never installed anything. All I know is maintenance. I think it takes a long time to put in a system, because they're very complicated." Milo wondered if the personal scanners hard to add to a system?" Bob looked at him as if he was speaking Chinese. "Personal scanners? I've never heard of those. What are they?" Milo asked, "What do you fix when you come here?" Bob looked at everyone. "Sometimes credit card machines go off-line. I don't know why, they just do. All I do is reconnect them to the systems."

Jordan looked at a very confused Bob and realized that he was only a fix-it guy. She asked, "How often do you have to service these systems?" Bob seemed to relax a little as he turned to Jordan. "We usually have calls about once a month, but lately, we've been at this hotel a lot." She pushed her glass of tea to Bob, "How long have you worked for this company?" Bob took a sip of the tea. "A little over a year." Jordan leaned over to Milo and whispered, "He doesn't have a clue about what's going on."

It took Mr. Cullen a little over fifteen minutes to get to the pub. He walked to the bar and Tim pointed him to the table in the corner. Bob's boss swaggered over to the table and said, "Bob, what seems to be the problem?" Charlie said, "We don't have a problem." The gruff little man in the not very expensive suit and tie said, "You do have a problem. Part of your system is off-line again. Let's talk in private." Charlie looked around the table and then back to Mr. Cullen. "This is the guy who told me if I didn't keep the scanners in place I could end up like Leroy, with a bullet in my brain." Mr. Cullen started to exit but couldn't because Milo was blocking his path. "Where are you going?" Charlie stood and introduced everyone. "This is Mr. and Mrs. Forbes, the owners of this hotel. This is Jordan Sutton and the guy behind you is her partner, Milo Starr. They're Private Investigators." CR stood and flashed his badge, "I'm CR Reid from the FBI. Sit down!" Tim shut the front door and put the closed sign on the pub.

The owner of CC Repair took a seat, looked around at everybody and in his best tough-guy accent said, "So, what's the occasion?" Charlie replied, "The hotel is pulling all the personal scanners today and these people are here to help." CR told him that using these scanners was a violation of both state and federal laws. "It also sounds as if you have information about the former Food and Beverage Manager's murder too." George Cullen's face was suddenly flushed. "I heard about Leroy's murder, but I didn't have nothin' to do with that." Charlie leaned into him and said, "But you told me if I didn't keep this scam going, my family would be alone on holidays. That scared the crap out of me."

Mr. Cullen got very silent, very quick. Milo asked, "What do you have to say about all this?" CR told him to start talking because right now he was the chief suspect in a murder and credit card fraud. Mr. Cullen said, "I don't know anything about that stuff." Jordan said, "I think it's time for you to tell us what you *do* know." Bob seemed really confused as he looked around the table. "Hey, I don't know what you're talking about. I don't know anything about a credit card scam."

Mr. Cullen looked at Jordan and then at the table and let out a deep breath. "Relax Bob, I'll take care of things. None of our employees know anything about the personal scanners. They just do repairs on the entire system. I'm not the guy running this thing. CC Repair just does the maintenance." Charlie got in his face. "Then why did you say that to me?" Mr. Cullen shrugged his shoulders, "That's what I was told to say. It's what I tell all the hotels to make sure everything keeps working."

Milo asked for a list of the other hotels they service, who pays them and how. CR glared at him, "Also, who's telling you to keep people in-line. Write it all down." Jordan put her notepad on the table and Mr. Cullen picked up her pen. "Will it help me to write everything?" CR said, "It couldn't hurt." Mr. Cullen began to write. CR watched him and said, "Put your name, address and phone number down too and show Jordan your driver's license."

When he finished writing, Mr. Cullen pushed the pad across the table and asked if he needed a lawyer? CR picked up the pad and looked over the info. "You don't need a lawyer if what you're telling us is the truth. You wrote that your company gets paid directly into your business checking account by a Z Corporation, is that correct?" Upon hearing that, Milo looked at Jordan and said, "Mr. Cullen do you know who runs the Z Corporation?" He shook his head and told them he didn't. "Everything was set up by phone and email." Charlie wanted to know if CC Repair set up all the hotels' systems. Mr. Cullen said, "No. We were hired about two years ago just to maintain everything at all five hotels. I don't know who installed the original systems or when."

Milo leaned over to him, "So, all the systems were already working?" Mr. Cullen nodded yes. "But you know what's going on, right? You know what they do with the personal scanners." George Cullen quietly said, "Yeah, I know now, but I didn't know anything in the beginning. We were just on-call for repair jobs. But once I learned what was going on I was told not to mention it to anyone. Just after Leroy's murder, I got a phone call telling me to keep things as they were, and I'd keep getting paid." Milo asked, "What would happen if you didn't keep the systems up and running?" Mr. Cullen got very serious and quiet. "They said I'd end up with a bullet in my head like Leroy Thomas, so I just kept going."

Mr. Cullen loosened his tie and looked around the table, "Do you really think you can end all of this?" Milo assured him that they could stop it at the Golden Oasis, "I don't know about the other hotels on your list." Jordan said, "If we stop it here, and arrest the people behind the scam, then it might end it everywhere." Mr. Cullen suddenly seemed very relieved. He looked at Jordan, "Okay, I believe you. How can I help?"

Everyone turned to Milo and Jordan for answers. Milo thought for a moment and then said, "Does anyone besides you know that the scanner in this bar is off-line right now?" George told them that only his office knows. "The people running this operation only learn about problems when they receive our invoices." Milo wanted to know when they got that information.

"If we're called out for a repair, the Z Corporation gets an invoice by the end of the month."

Milo smiled. "Here's what we'll do. Mr. Cullen, you go back to your office and don't mention that you had a call from this hotel. No one will know there's been any trouble here. Can you do that?" He nodded and said, "Yes, I can. I don't have to mention anything." CR said, "If you'll do that and keep all of this to yourself, I'm sure you won't be included in any criminal charges. I'm also sure you'll be safe." Mr. Cullen agreed, shook hands with everyone and turned to leave the pub. He seemed to be very relieved. Milo asked one more question. "Mr. Cullen who's your contact at this hotel? Who approves your invoices for work completed?" The owner of CC Repair stopped and looked at Milo. "We're paid by the Z Corporation after the invoice is approved by Sam Boyle, the hotel's G.M." James seemed surprised and asked, "Our General Manager signs off on your work?" George Cullen looked very confused and took his seat at the table again.

"Yes. Sam Boyle has been doing that for almost two years." Milo said, "We thought somebody inside the hotel was running this operation, but we didn't know who." Mr. Cullen seemed very agitated as he asked, "Does this put me and my family in danger?" CR said, "No. Nobody will know that we've talked. Just keep your mouth shut and you'll be safe." Mr. Cullen thanked them for their help and left quietly with a wave to Tim. Bob followed his boss and stopped to ask, "I'm not in any trouble, am I?" Milo told him he wasn't.

"Just keep doing your job, and don't mention this meeting and you'll be fine."

James sat back in his chair, "That wasn't what I expected." Milo agreed, "Tell me about your General Manager." James thought for a moment and said, "When our original GM, Ralph Watkins, retired we put out feelers for a replacement. It took us about two weeks to find Sam." James picked up the notepad and scanned the names of the hotels. "He was working as an assistant GM for one of the hotels on this list. I guess he wanted to move up." Kate said, "He had excellent references and we thought he was the right man for the job." Milo asked, "When did you hire him?" Neither of them could remember. "Charlie, do you remember when Sam came to work here?" Charlie didn't know either. Kate said, "I'm going to check." She excused herself to make a quick call to their personnel office.

Tim brought more tea to the table while they waited for Kate to return. Milo smiled and asked Charlie, "When do you expect Sam back on the job?" Charlie wasn't sure, "All I know is that he's on medical leave." Kate returned, and she wasn't smiling. "We hired Sam two years ago this week." James said, "That's about when the over-charging started." Kate sat next to her husband. "I guess we need a new General Manager." James nodded yes and looked at Milo. "What do we do next?"

Milo thought for a moment. "We have our morning meeting tomorrow with all the employees on Charlie's list and we'll tell them they are no longer allowed to use the scanners and see what happens. I think with both of you and CR in the room, they will get the message that it's over." James and Kate were hopeful that Milo was correct. Jordan smiled at Charlie as she said, "And let's not forget that tomorrow we 'arrest' Charlie and banish him and his family to Sleeping Beauty's Castle."

That brought a smile and laugh as they left the Pub. Charlie told Tim to remove his scanner. "We're not using them anymore." James and Kate thanked everyone for their help and told them to enjoy the hotel. Kate asked, "Have you been to our indoor pool?" Milo said they hadn't seen that, yet. Jordan announced it was Keno and slot machine time for her. Milo and CR were going to look for a friendly bar and then check out the pool area. James and Kate wished everyone good luck and said they would see everybody early tomorrow for the meeting.

CHAPTER 24

Staff Meeting

Milo opened the door to ballroom "C" and followed Jordan and CR into the room. James and Kate were seated with Charlie facing the employees' chairs, some of which were still empty. Charlie welcomed Jordan, Milo and CR and quietly said, "We're still waiting on a few. I'll give them another minute or two." Jordan and CR sat as Milo began to move around the room with his phone app set on SEARCH he was looking for electronic devices. The counter on the app registered seventy-two potential problems in the room. Several late-comers entered and took their seats and Milo's counter jumped to seventy-five. Charlie took a head count as the room got very quiet. He stood and asked them to turn off their cell phones. He paused while everyone complied then began to look over the list of things he needed to say.

"First, I want to thank all of you for coming this morning. I know some of you aren't scheduled for work and I'm sorry to interfere with your day off. Those that are on the work schedule today, we want you to know that you aren't late for your shift. We've taken care of that because this is an important meeting." Charlie turned toward their guests. "For those of you who are new to the job, I want you to meet the owners of the hotel, Mr. and Mrs. Forbes, next to them Jordan Sutton and Milo Starr, they're Private Investigators from Los Angeles and finally, CR Reid of the FBI." CR stepped forward and flashed his badge.

Milo noticed that everyone in the room suddenly looked very serious. Charlie continued, "I asked all of you to join us today and bring the personal scanner you've been using during your shift. Yes, all of you are using them. Milo could see that some were shocked at the announcement. He recalled that the bartender from the Pub mentioned he thought he was the only one using the device. Several seemed to know others were using them because they didn't react. Charlie continued, "As of today, we're disconnecting every scanner." He asked Jordan if she would collect the scanners and put them in the empty box on the floor. Almost everyone reacted to the news in some way. Some seemed shocked and others relieved as they removed their devices.

As Jordan walked around the room making sure that everyone put a device in the box, one man asked, "Are the units being replaced?" Charlie waited for the room to quiet down. "No, we're shutting down the entire system. The personal scanners will no longer be used at this hotel." A young lady spoke, "Mr. Brady, I was told that once I said yes to using the device, I couldn't quit. I've thought about quitting for a long time, but I was afraid to stop." Charlie understood, "I know. These systems have been in-place for a long time.

We have a plan to put an end to all of it. I would like Mr. and Mrs. Forbes to tell you how we're going to accomplish this."

James stepped forward. "Thank you Charlie and we want to thank all of you for joining us today. My wife and I learned about the overcharging several weeks ago. We found that our hotel has been paying off credit card companies who were alerted to the erroneous charges by some of our guests. After doing a full analysis of the extra charges, we've discovered that the hotel has paid out almost two-million-dollars. We had no idea how it was being carried out, so we asked for help from these two Private Investigators. Milo Starr and Jordan Sutton discovered the personal scanners."

Mr. Forbes stopped talking and looked around the room. "We know that each of you use these devices and as Charlie told you, as of today, we're no longer allowing their use." There was a little unrest in the small meeting room. James looked around the room and quietly said. "These scanner devices have cost us more than money." Kate added, "With each transaction, our hotel suffers a loss of integrity. Some clients might not trust us anymore. We may have lost business over the years." James added, "I believe there are many more charges that have never been reported because people didn't check their credit card statements. We can't afford to have that anymore. Everything stops today! We want you to know that none of you are at risk because we're shutting this system down. Only Charlie knows who was using the devices."

An older woman raised her hand and said, "I'm so glad to hear this is over. Some days, I didn't use the thing at all. I just felt it wasn't right." Mrs. Forbes moved next to her husband. "James and I are happy to hear that, thank you." The employee smiled. Kate continued, "We don't want any of you to lose your jobs. We know that many of you were doing this under duress and we're not going to allow the FBI to charge anybody." CR acknowledged Kate's announcement. He added, "What Mrs. Forbes said is true. You'll only be charged with fraud if you speak to anyone about what we're doing here. I'm on-site to observe the changeover and to make sure it goes smoothly."

Milo stood, "That's about it, except this. We've learned that the scanners are being used at other hotels too. We also surmise that you may know people at those hotels who use the devices. If you want to stay safe and out of the spotlight on this, don't talk to anyone about what we've discussed here today." Charlie added, "Don't tell anyone that the scanners are off-line, just go back to work and don't concern yourselves with any of this." He looked around the room. "If any of you have questions, we'll be here for a few minutes. We'll be glad to help you."

James and Kate thanked everyone for coming. James said, "Charlie, I'd like you to give all of these employees an hour of overtime for coming this morning." Charlie made a note and said he'd take care of it. Three employees remained and approached the front of the room. James and Kate asked them their names and job description. All of them were waiters, and they each had the same issues and concerns. They were worried about repercussions for stopping the charging. James explained again that nobody outside of this room knows who is using the scanners. "Remember, only Charlie knows your names." One employee said, "We want to thank you for not firing us or having anybody arrested." James told them that wouldn't be right. "You didn't start the scam you were just dragged into it."

They started to leave and one of the men said, "Mr. Forbes, when I started using the device, I thought it was great. After a while I wanted to quit using it, but Leroy said I couldn't stop. I think we were all scared when Leroy was killed and that's why we're really glad this is over." They all shook hands and cleared the room. James watched everyone leave. "I think that went well. We don't have to fire anybody." Kate agreed, and Charlie asked, "Now what?"

Milo stood and put his hands on Charlie's shoulders and said, "It's time to arrest you. Let's go to your office so everyone can hear what happens." Jordan looked at Charlie and smiled. "Now, we find out how good an actor you are." They left the conference room and entered the double doors which led to Charlie's office. Milo gave him his instructions. "Just go in and start working. We'll come in with CR and he'll arrest you. He'll make it seem that you're handcuffed and out we go." Charlie wanted to know if he should object. "Sure, say stuff like, what's the charge? I don't know what you're talking about. CR will tell you that if you tell him what you know, you'll get a reduced sentence. You ready?" Charlie nodded and entered his office.

Milo told Jordan that Charlie was nervous, "But I think he's ready." He told CR to make it sound like Charlie was really being handcuffed. Milo set his app to

SCAN as they entered the office. He motioned to Charlie to be quiet for a moment as he checked the area to make sure the office bugs were working. They were. Milo said, "Hi Charlie, remember us?" Charlie said, "Ahh… yes, Jordan Sutton and Milo Starr, the Private Investigators, what brings you back here?" Milo gave him a "thumbs-up" signal and looked at Jordan who said, "We're here for you Charlie. Well, not just us but our friend CR." CR took the cue. "Charlie Brady, I'm FBI agent CR Reid. You're under arrest for credit card fraud." Charlie waited for a moment and said, "Wait! I don't know what you're talking about." CR took out his cuffs and jiggled them and pretended to close them on Charlie who said, "Hey, that's too tight."

Milo gave him a smile and another "thumbs-up". CR said, "We might be adding to the charges once we get you to our office." Milo said, "Charlie, if you tell the FBI what you know, it could go easier on you." CR said, "That's right. Let's go." They exited the office as CR said, "You have the right to remain silent." The rights speech faded out as they entered the hallway and CR put the cuffs in his pocket. James and Kate who watched the play-acting from the hallway thought it was great. "Our limo is waiting outside at the rear of the casino." Kate said, "Thank you, Charlie. Have fun at Disneyland."

Charlie thanked them as he headed for the rear loading dock. Milo told him to have fun and not to worry about anything. Milo and Jordan looked around and didn't see anything that looked out of place. They opened the limo door for Charlie and he was happy to see his wife and two kids inside. They were all smiles and thanked Mr. and Mrs. Forbes. "We hope you have a nice vacation." Milo closed the limo door and waved as the happy family drove away.

CR said he was going to check with a good friend at the bureau in Las Vegas. "I want him to let me know if anybody asks about Charlie." Milo thought that was a good idea. Jordan said, "I think we had a good day, what do you think, Kate?" Mrs. Forbes thought it was an interesting day. "What are you doing tonight?" "I think we're going to take CR to your wonderful buffet." Jordan thanked Kate and told CR, "Let's go. I'm also teaching you how to play Keno." Milo wanted to know what time they would be flying back to L.A. James and Kate were talking quietly. James turned to the group. "Go play Keno for a while and then join us at the buffet at seven. We have a private, reserved area." Milo loved that idea. He looked at Jordan and CR who were both happy with the selection. "OK, we'll see you at seven."

Keno was fun. Everybody had at least one winning ticket during the session. When the cocktail waitress came by, they all ordered and when CR found out the drinks were free he said, "I think Keno is my favorite game." They continued to play and drink until it was time to dress for dinner. "We'll see you at seven." Milo and Jordan went up to their suite. "You didn't bring five suitcases, what are you going to wear tonight?" She dismissed his comment, "Don't worry about me. What are *you* wearing?" Milo said he had a nice evening outfit. He asked her if she wanted to shower first. "No, you go first." Milo wasted no time heading to the exquisite bathroom. He shaved and took a nice relaxing shower. Jordan passed him with a quick kiss as she entered the bedroom area.

He opened his suitcase and removed a pair of black slacks and a black aloha shirt with small palm trees embroidered in black. He was officially black on black on black. As he fixed a gin and tonic from their bar, he took a call from Carol and strolled over to the very large window as he talked. The super-bright neon and high-def billboard skyline of the Vegas strip was beautiful. "Yes Carol, we're fine. No, nobody is shooting at us. We'll be flying back tomorrow. See you at the office on Monday." Milo ended the call and turned toward the bedroom area of the suite. Jordan had just emerged from the changing area. "Wow, where did you get that outfit?"

She paraded around the bed and met him in the living room. "Do you like it?" Milo took a swallow of his drink. "Yes, I love it, but where did it come from?" "Kate sent it over while you were in the shower. It fits me perfectly. Kate is my new style guru. Shall we go?" Milo thought she looked fantastic, but he knew he had to thank Kate for her selection. The silver mid-calf dress looked great next to Milo's black on black ensemble. Jordan flashed her special ring and pointed to the necklace that the Forbes' bought her on their last trip.

They stepped out of the elevator and heads began to turn. "I think people like my basic black look." Jordan laughed, "Yes, they're all looking at you and wondering how you landed this classy girl?" She took his arm and they strolled across the casino floor heading for the executive entrance of the Oasis Buffet.

During dinner, James and Kate wanted to hear how Jordan and Milo met and became partners. Milo turned that part of the evening over to Jordan who loved telling the story of their college friendship and how Milo helped her when a bunch of bad cops were trying to kill her. She also brought their long-time friendship with CR into the conversation. James said, "We remember Mr. Reid from the press conferences. You're the person who gave credit to Sutton and Starr for solving the mutilation murders." Kate said, "That's one of the reasons we called them." James raised his wine glass, "And, it was the best call we ever made."

CR smiled, "Then I guess you owe me a percentage of your fee." Milo raised his glass to CR and said, "In your dreams FBI boy." CR laughed and said he was only kidding. "I'm glad I could assist in this operation." Kate raised her glass to CR, "You're a pretty good actor too. We'll fly back tomorrow about four, how's that?" That was a perfect time for everyone.

Their conversation was interrupted when Milo's phone buzzed. He looked and retrieved a text message. Milo said. "I just got a text from CC Repair. *When I got back to the office, I asked our bookkeeper Tina, to print out a few things I thought might help you. I'll leave it at the hotel desk a little later. George Cullen - CC Repair*"

CHAPTER 25

Help is on the Way

Milo raised his beer mug. "Looks like we might be getting help. CC Repair is sending over some papers." James and Kate thanked everyone for helping them as Kate said, "I think we'll head upstairs." She smiled at Jordan, "We need to unwind. It's been a crazy day." Jordan smiled back, "We'll be doing the same thing a little later." James told everyone to sit and finish their drinks. "We'll see you tomorrow afternoon." Kate took her husband's arm and headed for the elevator. She glanced back at Jordan, smiled and raised her eyebrows. Ms. Sutton smiled back and understood Kate's code for "unwind." They were going to play the honeymoon game.

CR was looking around, "This is a beautiful hotel." He turned to Sutton and Starr. "You guys have a great job." Milo laughed, "Yes, this is a good assignment, but remember ninety-nine percent of what we do is not this glamorous." Jordan ran her hand up Milo's arm. "Or fun." Milo grinned, "Finish your drinks. I want CR to see more of the hotel." Milo took Jordan's arm and they started to wander toward RDN, the hotel's shopping district. CR couldn't believe they were still in the hotel, "I feel like I'm back in Beverly Hills. The only things missing are the cars." Jordan laughed and dragged CR into her favorite jewelry store. "Why don't you buy a present for your bride-to-be?" CR looked over several cases and said he would consider buying something, if he won some money.

Milo received a text from the front desk. "There's an envelope for us, let's go pick it up, then we'll have a few more drinks." Jordan took his arm. "Wow, you're buying drinks?" Milo smiled and retrieved a blank Keno ticket from his pocket. "Nah not me, drinks are on the hotel." They walked and gawked at the opulence of the building and as they approached the front desk, the concierge stood to greet them. "Good evening Mr. and Mrs. Starr. This envelope is for you. I hope you're enjoying your stay with us." Jordan smiled and told the very soft-spoken young lady that they loved everything about the hotel and the staff. Milo thanked her for the envelope as they headed for the Keno lounge only to find that the place was packed. There wasn't an empty chair in the lounge. Milo said, "Okay, let's head to the Mexican bar. We can play there because they have Keno runners."

They found a table facing the remote Keno board and when asked what they wanted Jordan said, "It's Margarita time with salt." Their waiter asked if they would like some guacamole too. Jordan, who dug right into the chips and salsa replied, "Yes, that would be great." Milo opened the 9 x12 envelope and removed a small stack of pages. He handed half to Jordan. They both looked over the information and each one started to smile. CR watched them and asked, "Why are you smiling?"

Milo started to talk but stopped when the drinks and avocado dip arrived. "Will you need anything else?" Jordan said, "Not right now." Milo looked around and told CR what was in the printouts. "There's a note from Tina the bookkeeper at CC Repair. She says, *"Mr. Cullen said you needed data about who pays us for work at the five hotels. He said there was something bad going on, so I wanted to help. If you need more info, please call me. Tina."* CR put down his drink and asked, "Okay, what did she send?"

Jordan was reading and licking the salt off the rim of her drink. "Well, here's a photocopy of a check from the Z Corporation that pays invoice number 2205. They have a PO Box in Marina Del Rey." Milo looked through his papers and said, "I found invoice 2205 for one-thousand dollars. It's for repair work at The Golden Oasis and the invoice was approved by the General Manager, Sam Boyle. So, he is involved, for sure."

CR asked if there was anything there about how to find the Z Corporation. Milo showed CR a copy of an email in which Z Corp asked CC Repair to ship them a personal scanner. CR raised his drink, "Looks like you got 'em." Milo also raised his glass, "You might be right. All we have to do is search the address, then move in for an arrest." CR laughed, "I'll bet it's going to be a little harder than that."

The trio drank, snacked and played Keno in the Mexican restaurant. Their very attentive Keno runner kept them playing till the wee hours of the morning.

Each of them won a few dollars playing the game, but playing this way and not in the lounge meant they didn't get free drinks. They talked over the information they currently had, and the overall feeling was that they had the ammo to stop the crimes now; it was just a matter of doing things in the right order to bring it all to an end. Milo and Jordan headed to the elevators telling CR not to stay out too late. "Breakfast buffet is at nine. We'll see you there."

CR turned toward the Keno lounge as the elevator doors closed. Milo checked his watch. "It's almost three AM. Are you tired?" She pushed him against the elevator wall and kissed him with the enthusiasm of a teenager. He gasped for air and whispered, "Wow, I guess you're not tired." The elevator stopped at their floor and she led him across the hall. "You better not be too tired either." He opened the door and she kissed him again. Milo knew he was in for a short, but wonderful night.

CHAPTER 26

What Happens in Vegas...

Milo's phone woke him with its familiar buzz. He found it on the charger and retrieved a text from James Forbes. ***"We have meetings this morning. Can't locate our GM. The limo will pick us up at 4:30. Meet in front lobby. We'll see you then."*** Milo stretched and looked over at his sleeping partner. He smiled and thought, *"Nothing bothers her sleep time."* He slipped on his elegant hotel robe, as he trudged to the bathroom for a quick shave and shower. The next order of business was to say hello to the pod coffee maker. After the appliance did its thing, he took the great-tasting dark brew to the couch in the living room area of their suite and slowly opened the blackout curtains. He was greeted with a pre-sunrise view of the Las Vegas Strip. There wasn't much traffic on the street, but it looked like the start of a wonderful day.

He called Carol. "Good morning." Carol wanted to know what was wrong. "Are you okay?" Milo told her they were fine. "I just got up early and wanted to tell you that we'll be flying in later today." She was glad to hear they weren't in trouble. "I'll see you in the office, when?" Milo yawned and said, "Not tomorrow. We need a vacation after this job." Carol said, "Okay boss, I'll see you Tuesday. I have a long list of calls for you and Jordan to make."

Milo ended the conversation and was about to wake Jordan for breakfast when he noticed the papers from CC Repair on the coffee table. It was very quiet— a perfect time to read over the data again. It only took a few minutes for Milo to realize that they needed a few more pieces of information to continue. He sent a text to George Cullen, **"Did anybody at CC Repair ever meet anyone from the Z Corporation?"**

It was time to drag Jordan out of bed and point her toward the bathroom. "Time to get going young lady. After last night, I'm starving." She kissed him on the cheek as she closed the bathroom door. Milo called CR and found he was already in the casino playing a few slots. He said he was winning. "I'll meet both of you at the buffet in an hour."

Breakfast was so wonderful Jordan didn't want to leave the table. She also didn't want to leave the hotel and get back to normal life. "This place has really spoiled me." Milo agreed. "Are you packed?" She smiled and took the last bite of her jelly donut. "As a matter of fact, I am." Milo was shocked. "Where is your bag?" She finished her coffee, "My bag is right next to yours in the suite." "Wow, I can't believe it." She got up, put a five-dollar bill on the table and said, "I'm off, video poker and Keno are calling." Milo and CR finished their coffee and followed her into the casino. Milo stopped short as his cell phone received a text from James. *"A few things have come up, we can't leave until six PM. See you then."* He told Jordan and CR about the change of plans. Both of them, almost in unison said, "Great" as they headed to the Keno lounge.

Milo wandered around the casino and stopped at the Roulette wheel where a game was in progress. He waited and was about to place a one-hundred dollar bet on number seventeen on the next game when the ball dropped, and the Croupier announced, "Seventeen, black odd." Milo stopped and thought, *"It won't hit twice in a row."* He noticed a large five-dollar slot machine across the aisle from the Roulette table and decided to put his hundred-dollar bill in the machine. It had a massive LED screen but was still a standard-looking slot machine with many different "7's. Some were red, others blue and many had stars, and some had red chilies. There were some double and triple chili icons also with the number 7. He began to play the first of his twenty games as the Croupier announced, "Seventeen, black odd." Milo thought, *"Oh, well, I was wrong."* As his machine displayed two sevens and he made ten dollars.

It wasn't the thirty-five-hundred he would have won at Roulette, but he still smiled and kept playing his giant "Triple Red-Hot Chili" slot machine. The 7's kept coming. Some screens showed two red that paid a little more, others were scrambled 7's that didn't line up so, no payout. Milo looked at his remaining $20 and decided to double up and played ten dollars on the next pull. The 7's spun around and locked in this way: Double RED Chili 7, Double RED Chili 7 and the final window displayed a third Double RED Chili 7. The machine lit up and the payout music began. He looked at the legend above to see what he'd won and felt a little self-conscious as the music and graphic coins cascaded across the screen. He had a hard time figuring out what he won because of all the flashing graphics. After what seemed like a long time the machine completed its payout cycle. The CASHOUT button kept flashing, so he pressed it.

The machine dispensed a voucher for thirteen-thousand-five-hundred dollars. He retrieved the voucher and turned to leave but he encountered a smiling slot attendant behind him who checked the I.D. number of the machine and called in the win. "Congratulations, you can redeem that voucher at the cage." She then pointed out that he had ten dollars credit in the machine. "Play it." Milo played one credit and won another twenty dollars and didn't win on his final play. He cashed out the twenty dollars and thanked the slot attendant for noticing. "That's my job. You would be surprised at how many times people think they're finished but they aren't." The attendant had a call and was told to accompany Milo to the main cashier's cage, "Walk with me please." They walked to the other side of the casino and she handed the cashier a note with the machine's I.D. number and the amount of the win. She smiled and congratulated Milo again.

He filled out the IRS form and was asked if he wanted cash or a check. He asked if he could have three-thousand-five-hundred in cash and the balance in a check? The cashier said, "Yes, we do that all the time." She took his paperwork, excused herself and went to get his check. Milo was happy he didn't play Roulette today, but he also knew that if he mentioned his big win to Jordan she'd hound him for a present. He was smiling as the cashier returned with his cash and check. "Thank you for playing here at the Golden Oasis. I know you're enjoying your stay because winners always do." Milo thanked her and was smiling as he walked toward the Keno lounge.

CR and Jordan were watching the Keno board, as twenty floating numbered balls were picked. Jordan was smiling, "Hey, I won two-dollars." Milo smiled, "That's great. I had a winner too." CR asked, "Yeah, what did you win?" Milo took out the wad of cash. "Thirty-five-hundred on a slot machine." Jordan suddenly got very lovey-dovey. "Well big boy, what are you going to do now?" Milo hugged his partner and then pulled away. "I just realized what I'm going to do. I'm going to keep my mouth shut from now on, if I win anymore." Jordan laughed and whacked him with her Keno ticket. "You'll buy me a present, you know you will." She was right, he would add something for Carol too.

Once inside the private jet, Milo showed James and Kate the file from CC Repair. They quickly looked over the data and asked, "Do you think this will help you find out who's behind this?" Jordan said she thought it would. Milo agreed. "Once we get to my computer system I think I'll probably be able to figure it out." James and Kate were extremely appreciative for everyone's help. "CR what can we do for you to say thanks?" The FBI agent told them that he was just there to help Milo and Jordan, "And enjoy your beautiful hotel and steakhouse, of course." Jordan had an idea. She took Kate aside and spoke softly to her.

Kate turned to CR. "'Jordan tells me you're getting married soon. Do you have a date picked?" CR said they didn't, his lady was still deciding. "But soon, I hope." Kate asked about the location. CR told them that they really didn't have that figured out either. She smiled, "Would you like to have the ceremony at our hotel? We have beautiful wedding chapels." Jordan loved the idea, "What do you think, CR?" The agent, who always seemed to have an answer to everything wasn't sure. "Can I get back to you on that?" Kate handed him her business card and told him to call when he had an answer. Jordan told her that she would make sure he got back to her.

When they landed, there were hugs all around. James and Kate couldn't thank everyone enough. Milo told them that he would call them the instant they had new information. Their limos were waiting, and they soon parted company. As they rode toward their condo Jordan thanked CR for being with them and reminded him to call Kate when he had plans for the wedding. He said he would. Milo added, "Getting hitched at their hotel will save you a bundle." Jordan laughed, "Plus, it gives us a reason to go back to Las Vegas."

Once inside their condo Milo turned on his computer system, Jordan called Carol and they yacked for several minutes. "We'll see you Tuesday." She hung up and said, "Did you buy Carol a gift?" Milo was busy with his computer but managed to say, "Yes, it's in my carry-on. I'll show it to you later." Jordan began to unpack but stopped and fixed two glasses of wine.

When she set one on Milo's computer desk, he asked, "What's this for?" She sat on the couch, "I just felt like saying I love you with wine." Milo joined her and clinked glasses. "I kind of love you too." She lightly kicked him on the shin. "What did you get Carol?" He motioned toward his bag. "Hand me my carry-on and I'll show you."

His small leather bag was next to the couch, so she didn't have to move to hand it to him. He looked and removed two small boxes from RDN Diamonds. He handed her one box. "I got her a bracelet." Jordan opened the box. "She'll love this. What's in the other box?" Milo tried not to smile as he answered, "It's a little something I picked up for my girlfriend." Milo laughed, "Take a look and tell me if you think she'll like it." Jordan slowly opened the second box and discovered another diamond bracelet.

"Wow, it's beautiful." Milo took a sip of his wine. "So, you think she'll like it?" Jordan kept playing the game. "Yes, I think she'll love it." Milo finished his wine. "Okay, then why don't you wear it until I see her again?" Jordan removed the beautiful piece and hit Milo with the box. "Thank you, it's beautiful." She hugged and kissed him on the cheek. "I'll take good care of it for her. Now, I need a boyfriend to take me somewhere, so I can wear it." They both smiled and hugged again.

Milo left his computer doing a deep information search for Z Corporation. Each search was leading him nowhere. He was running into firewalls protected by even stronger firewalls. He tried one more idea. He lined up nine servers in as many countries, in an attempt to mask his search. He left the program running as he started toward the bedroom, "I'm tired. Let's watch TV in bed." Jordan carried her new bracelet to the bedroom. "I think we need to put this beauty in the safe." Milo said he would tomorrow. "Tonight, just wear it to bed." Jordan smiled and hopped in next to Milo who kissed her on the cheek and pretended to nod off. "Sorry mister, but you're not sleeping much tonight." Milo smiled, opened his eyes and snuggled with his lover. He kissed her and began to gently caress her backside when his computer system beeped. She asked, "What was that?" Milo kissed her again and whispered, "Just the computer, we'll check it in the morning." Jordan smiled and loved his massage.

CHAPTER 27

The Search

Milo was still half-asleep as he dragged his butt to the kitchen and started to make coffee. His next stop was the computer. The late-night search was completed, but not successful. He sipped his dark-roast as he read the search results. **Z Corporation - no results found**! He moved to the sliding glass door and opened it a crack. There was a slight chill in the air and his mind was zooming a million miles an hour as he analyzed what he would have to do to locate the people running the scams. Something didn't feel right. What was missing? Then it hit him. He needed his whiteboard and the ability to post everything about the case on the wall. Then he could walk and think. It's what Jordan and Carol called his "Milo Thing."

He also realized that he would have to do some serious hacking to learn more about this mysterious corporation. He pulled out the info from CC Repair and looked it over again. He used a large magnifying glass to read the routing number on the check that Z Corporation sent to CC Repair Company. The copy wasn't very clear, but he began to search the number which wasn't correct. He tried another variation of the routing number. It took Milo several tries to find the location of the account, but he couldn't access the information from the front door because he didn't have the username and password. That just meant he would have to attempt to enter through the back door, if he could find one.

Jordan, wearing her fuzzy robe, joined Milo in the living room. "You're up early. Why?" He turned away from the monitor and tried not to laugh when he saw his half-awake partner with extremely messy morning hair. "I'm searching for the Z Corporation. It kind of kept me awake last night." She yawned, "How far did you get?" Milo turned back to the computer. "Not very far." She mumbled, "You need to do your Milo thing? Get moving! Get walking and thinking." Milo laughed and realized they both had the same thoughts. He tempted her with a sumptuous breakfast on the way to the office. She stopped, "You said we weren't working until tomorrow." He turned back to the monitor, "I know, but we could go eat and then slip into the office and not be bothered by phone calls or anything. Carol has the phone forwarded to her home." Jordan loved the idea of a big breakfast and a quiet day. She hurried to dress before he changed his mind.

At a fashionable business address across town, a well-dressed gentleman approached the secretary's desk. "Hello, I'm Gino and I have an appointment." The secretary smiled and dialed her boss. While she waited for a response, she gave the very muscular gentleman a fast once-over. "Mr. Z, Gino is here to see you." *"Please, send him in."* Gino, the polite but tough-looking gentleman, entered the office. "Good morning Mr. Z." "Good morning Gino, coffee?" Mr. Z pointed toward the coffee pot and Gino took him up on the suggestion. "Nice suit." Gino acknowledged the compliment as he poured his cup of the espresso brew and took a seat in front of the shiny uncluttered desk.

Mr. Z looked at his imposing guest, "Gino, I have a problem. I received several emails last week with audio clips attached, but they all went into my junk mail folder. I just found them yesterday. They were all recorded at a hotel in Vegas. In one clip, the Food and Beverage guy is talking to two Private Investigators from Los Angeles. This is serious stuff. I have an operation in place in Vegas that seems to be going south because of these two private dicks. Give a listen." Mr. Z hit play.

> *"Come in please, I remember your name is Jordan, but ah…She's Jordan Sutton and I'm Milo Starr. Here's our card." "You're private Investigators?" "Yes, we've been hired by the owners to investigate the massive credit card over-billing going on in the hotel."*

Mr. Z closed the file and looked at Gino. He opened Sutton & Starr's website and turned the monitor around. "They have offices right here in West L.A." Gino said he knew their names because they solved a big case recently. "They got lots of publicity." Mr. Z copied their contact information and sent it to his printer. "I have a great operation going on now and then these two clowns are getting in the way. They're costing me big money."

Mr. Z handed the two-page printout to Gino who looked at the photo of the detectives posed under the sign on the front of their building. "Sutton and Starr Private Investigators. What do you want done with them?" Mr. Z looked across the desk and quietly said, "I want them dead!" Gino folded one page, put it in his inside pocket and took a final sip of his coffee. "It will take me a few days to get their patterns down, but I will get it done. How much is involved in your Vegas deal?"

"They're gonna cost me about twenty-five-million." Gino was very matter-of-fact in his response. "Okay, then it's a hard hit for sure. I'll take care of both of 'em." Mr. Z handed him an envelope. "Here's some cash to get you started. More when the job's finished. That should scare the crap out of the hotel owners and keep things as they are. If not, you'll get more work." Gino stood, put the envelope in the inside pocket of his jacket without counting it, and thanked Mr. Z. "We'll talk soon." He exited the office leaving Mr. Z alone. After a moment or two, the boss grabbed the website printout, crumbled it and threw it against the wall.

CHAPTER 28

Long Week Ahead

The instant they entered the reception area Carol jumped up to welcome them back and then said, "I think we had a break-in here." Milo stopped and turned to Carol and tried not to laugh. "Why do you say that?" She opened the door to his office. "Well, look at this place, it's a mess. Someone put papers all over the floor; they must have been looking for something. I didn't do it." Milo couldn't hold it anymore and started laughing as he entered his office.

Jordan told Carol that they popped in yesterday, so Milo could do his walk and talk to himself thing. "Nobody broke-in." Carol was relieved and then began to chatter non-stop as she bombarded Jordan with a million questions. "Tell me everything about your adventure." Jordan knew that her job was to give Carol the story. Not the full story but just enough. The ladies took seats on the couch in Milo's office as he opened the sliding wall panel and began to write on the hidden whiteboard. He picked up a few papers from the floor and posted them.

Jordan talked about the hotel, the spa, the sump-tuous buffet, the shopping and the Keno Lounge. "What about your room?" Jordan showed her a few photos of their suite and then found a bunch of food shots from various restaurants. Jordan said they might have to return. Carol asked, "Can I join you guys the next time you go?" Milo was too busy to listen to the gab-fest. He was printing out information from his searches and posting the data from CC Repair. He stood back to look at the array of data on the wall behind the sliding panel and began to slowly pace around the office.

The ladies left him walking and talking to himself. Carol said, "I have better things to do than watch Mr. Starr wear a hole in the carpet." Jordan headed to her office to work on her callback list. Milo kept thinking, walking and talking to himself for several hours. He wrote this question on the whiteboard and kept underlining it each time he asked himself the question. *"Why did Z Corporation want the hotel to send them a scanner?"* He wrote that on the board again, larger with many question marks around it. Lunchtime came and went, and Milo was still doing his thing.

Carol interrupted his walking and talking to ask how many calls he made from his list. He didn't answer. Jordan looked in to say she was halfway through with her callback list; he didn't respond. "I'm also hungry and naked." Once again, he just kept looking at his board. He stopped and noticed Jordan's shadow on the carpet. "Sorry, I was thinking. Did you ask me something?" She took a seat in his desk chair,

"Yes, I asked how many calls you made and mentioned that I'm really hungry!"

Milo picked up his callback list and noticed that about half of the calls were requests for interviews. "Jordan, do you have any interview requests on your list?" She looked quickly, "Yes, I have three." Milo dropped his list on the desk, "What do they want to ask us that we haven't already answered?" Jordan shrugged her shoulders. "I don't know. I have a better question for you, where are we eating dinner?"

Milo grinned, "Let's go to the buffet. I love the way they do the prime rib." Jordan laughed and offered an alternative since they were no longer in Las Vegas. "Do you think they serve prime rib at Jordan's Steakhouse? If not, they have many other tasty choices and you can also drink because, you don't have to drive." Milo liked that idea and told her to let him know when. She dropped her call list on his desk. "I'm ready now." They told Carol they would finish their calls tomorrow. "Let's get out of here early-ish today." Carol didn't have to be asked twice. She was ready and headed to her desk to shut off her computer.

Milo stopped and looked at Jordan. He closed the wall panel, "Here's what I've got so far. We have a murder. We've stopped the scanners and right now, because CC Repair hasn't notified Z Corporation, nobody knows they aren't scanning." Jordan asked if Milo had returned any calls. "Not yet, but I will. I can't focus on that stuff right now. What about you? Who did you call?" Jordan checked her notes. "I spoke with a lady and her husband who want to see if we can vet her daughter's fiancé. They think he might be a little shady.

Does that sound like something we should do?" Milo thought it might be an easy case. Jordan agreed.

"Did you give Carol her gift?" Milo shook his head, "No, it's here." He reached in his briefcase and handed her the box from RDN Diamonds. "You give it to her." Jordan gladly took the gift and enter the reception area. "Carol, we really appreciate what you do around here, so Milo picked up a little something that you're probably going to love." Carol took the box. "Oh my, where is RDN Diamonds?" Jordan explained that it was at the Golden Oasis Hotel. "That's the place that's owned by our clients, Mr. and Mrs. Forbes. Milo won playing a slot machine and bought both of us presents." She extended her right hand. "I got this ring, and this is yours." Carol opened the box and couldn't believe her eyes. "Wow, this is beautiful. It's all diamonds. I've never had anything like this before." She leaned into Milo's office. "Thank you, boss." He smiled, "You're welcome. I thought it was better than a t-shirt or a mug that says I heart Las Vegas." She grinned back at him, "Yes, this is so much better. I hope you're going back to gamble more." Milo put a few files in his briefcase and said, "Let's get out of here." He shut down his computer. "Carol, we'll see you in the morning." Carol put her new treasure in her purse and smiled all the way home.

Milo started his car and looked at Jordan. He continued to stare without saying a word. "What? What's wrong?" Milo took her hand. "Nothing's wrong and that's what's wrong. We just worked a lot of hours and you look as fresh as you did this morning." She leaned over and kissed him on the cheek. "Thanks for the compliment. Home, please." They headed out of the parking garage. Jordan removed her heels and settled into the soft leather seat. He knew she'd be snoozing in a few minutes. They were zipping along and never noticed the nondescript car following them to their condo.

They parked in their reserved space as Jordan opened her eyes. Milo said, "Before you ask, yes, you were sleeping. After that drive, I need a drink. Let's just head to the bar." Jordan was also ready for food, so they hurried down the block. The owner, Mr. Jordan welcomed them and told the bartender to give them each a drink on the house.

Milo was smiling, "Thank you, Mr. Jordan. Can we each have a Mai Tai, please?" "You sure can. I saw a short story about your exploits in the paper this morning. I'm glad you came in because I wanted to thank you for solving the city-wide murders. Look around, we've had great business like this for the entire month. On the weekends, we even have a waiting list. People are once again going out to eat." Milo looked and counted six at the bar and only two empty tables in the dining room. "We're glad you're doing so well." The owner escorted them to a semi-private table and pulled out the chair for Jordan. "Thank you." The hostess put the menus on the table as the bartender delivered their drinks and Jordan was doing what she did everywhere they went, she was counting people. She and Milo usually knew how many bodies were near them.

Milo was reading his menu, not counting. Jordan finished her count and had to add one because a rather large, muscular man pulled up a bar stool. Milo removed the umbrella from his Mai Tai and tilted it to Jordan. She did the same back to him. "I'm going to be on the computer tonight for a while." She wanted to know what he'd be doing. He raised his glass to his partner. "Not telling. We'll chalk it up to plausible deniability. They always say that in spy movies. That way, you won't have to lie, if I get caught." She raised her glass to him. "Me? I wouldn't say anything to anybody."

Milo picked up the menu, started to read it again and peeked over the top. "What are you eating?" Before she could answer, their waiter placed a large Caesar Salad in the center of the table. "Compliments of the house." Jordan smiled at the waiter and asked him to thank the owner. "Shall we dig in?" They had another lovely, relaxing evening complete with piano music in the background. What they didn't pay any attention to, was the rather large, well-dressed man seated at the bar. Gino was watching S & S and was ready to zero in on the duo.

During dinner, James called to say that he and Kate were going back to the hotel. "We just received a call from Charlie. The police contacted him because they found the body of our GM, Sam Boyle." Jordan watched as Milo got very quiet. "How did it happen?" James didn't know much but it seemed to the authorities that it was murder. Jordan stopped eating as Milo said, "If you need us, just call." She wanted to know what was going on? "They think Sam Boyle was murdered. It has to be connected to this mess." Jordan said, "Now we have two murders." Their waiter replaced their drink glasses with a new round of Mai Tai's. Jordan said, "Thank you. If I drink this, will you carry me home?" Milo nodded but didn't speak very much as they finished their drinks and dinner.

Mr. Jordan met Sutton and Starr on their way out the front door. They thanked him for the drinks and the salad. He said it was just his way of saying thanks for helping the city get back to normal. As they walked, Jordan said, "I don't know why I feel sad about Sam Boyle, we didn't even know him." Milo held her close. "I feel bad for James and Kate. They knew him and now they have to hire someone to replace him." S & S hugged and kissed as they sort-of staggered their way home.

They were following several other diners up the quaint street who were chatting about the great food and service. Gino exited the bar and was walking about ten paces behind the duo with his hand on his weapon when a police car rolled slowly down the block. Milo and Jordan smiled and waved at the two cops and continued up the block toward their condo. Mr. Z's henchman turned and headed back in the direction of the restaurant's parking lot.

As soon as they got home, Milo set the alarm and turned his attention to his secure computer system. Jordan kept watching him as she washed her hands and poured two glasses of wine. It took a little over an hour, for Milo to complete his cyber break-in. He sat back and seemed relaxed. Jordan asked if he did it. Milo finished his wine, "I did, but I didn't learn much. We may never find out who's behind this operation." He closed his system and stretched. Jordan asked if he wanted a neck rub. Milo grinned from ear-to-ear. "You didn't have to ask." She began to rub his neck and shoulders. He told her that tomorrow he would make all the calls on his list including the interview inquiries. She stopped the neck rub. "What changed your mind?" He smiled, "Well, tonight, we got free drinks and a nice salad. James and Kate hired us because of an interview we did so, who knows, maybe with more stories, we'll get more business. She agreed and added, "Some P.I. firms and lawyers have to make TV commercials to get business. We've been lucky." She continued his neck massage. "Tell me when you're ready for bed." Milo didn't answer so she grabbed his hand and dragged him to the bedroom.

On a scale from one to ten, tonight's action between the sheets was a twelve! Jordan went to sleep smiling. Milo was smiling for a while, but he couldn't shut off his brain. He didn't know if they were going to be able to solve this case.

CHAPTER 29

Are you Jordan Sutton?

Over the next few days Sutton and Starr were constantly on the phone setting up interviews and meetings with new clients because Milo finally understood how important free publicity is to the life of their business. Jordan told Mr. S that she talked with an industry magazine who wanted to do an in-depth interview with them. Milo put down his phone, "If you think we should do it then let's do it. Just tell me when. What else did you find in your calls?" Jordan gave him a short run-down. "I talked with the lady that wants us to do the vetting of her daughter's fiancé." "When?" Jordan said they had been emailing back and forth and she set up the meeting for that afternoon. Carol buzzed, *"You have a call from Mr. Forbes."* Milo picked up the phone. "Hi, James, what's up?"

"Milo. We're in Las Vegas and we've got trouble again. Charlie was threatened over the phone and then again in our parking garage. The police want to talk to us about our GM. It will be a short conversation because we don't know anything. Are you any closer to finding out who's behind this?" Jordan could tell by

Milo's expression that the news wasn't good. "We're close, but we need a little more time. Do you want us to come up there?" James told him that wouldn't be necessary right now. Milo explained that they were still working to identify the person or persons running the operation. "Jordan and I will call you the instant we have something." He put down the phone, looked at his partner and relayed the phone conversation. "Can you take the meeting with the mother today?" Jordan said, "Sure. What are you going to do?"

He thought for a moment and quietly said, "I'm going to break the law again. I need to find out who owns and runs the Z Corporation and it really is best if you're not around. Carol should go home too. Tell her to take off early." Jordan turned toward the door. "Will do. Let me have your keys, I'll leave you alone to do your thing." Milo checked his desk for the keys. Jordan said, "I'll go see the mother. I should be back in an hour or so. Does that give you enough time?" He nodded yes and as she turned to leave Milo found the keys in his pocket. He tossed them to her as she headed into the lobby saying, "Do me a favor Mr. S please don't get caught." She was playing with Milo's keys as she told Carol to take off early and go hug her kids. "I'm going to interview a new client. Here's her address and phone number. We'll see you tomorrow." Milo yelled, "Drive safely, I'd like the car back in one piece." Jordan laughed, "One piece? That's no fun." She closed the door and turned toward the elevator. Carol didn't waste any time. She straightened her desk and looked in on Milo. "Jordan said I should go home and hug my kids. Do you need anything before I leave?" "Nope, see you tomorrow." Carol shut off her computer and she and her purse headed to the elevator. Two ladies were waiting to go to the parking garage. Carol yelled, "Hold the elevator, please." They waited for Carol who asked if they were going to lunch? "No, we're going home early."

Jordan stepped off the elevator and was smiling as she walked to Milo's car. She tossed his keys in the air and was looking forward to driving; it had been a while since she was behind the wheel. A strong male voice asked, "Are you Jordan Sutton?" She caught the keys, turned around and came face-to-face with a tall stocky man in a hoodie and his 9mm handgun. She started to turn to her left and reached for her weapon, as he fired. His bullet hit Jordan low on her right side. The stinging pain caused her to twist to her right as his second shot tore into her left shoulder, a millimeter from her heart. Both injuries occurred in a matter of seconds. She dropped the car keys and her purse as she slumped to the ground. Gino looked at his target bleeding on the concrete floor and approached the body to put a third shot in the back of her head, as the elevator doors opened.

The three passengers were laughing as they stepped into the parking garage. They continued to talk to Carol as she hit the unlock button on her key fob. The BEEP-BEEP of her car alarm startled Gino who stopped moving. He removed the silencer from his weapon and quickly left the garage. Carol yelled to her friends, "See you all tomorrow." As she opened her car door she noticed that Milo's convertible hadn't moved. "Jordan? Are you still here?" She approached Milo's car and screamed at the bloody scene she found. "*What do I do?"* Carol fumbled with her phone and called the office. Between the tears, she managed to tell Milo what happened. He asked Carol to call 911 and left the office flying down the three flights of stairs to the parking garage.

Moments later he was at Jordan's side kneeling on the garage floor. He lifted her gently and checked to see if she was breathing. "Did you call 911?" Carol said she did. He ripped a piece from the bottom of his shirt and used it to press against her shoulder wound which was bleeding profusely. Milo hoped the bullet had missed the heart as he hugged her and stroked her bloody hair. Carol gave him a handkerchief from her purse and he pressed it into the lower torso wound. He rocked his bleeding partner slowly in his arms.

The EMT crew and Fire Department arrived in a matter of minutes but in Milo's mind, it was an hour. They were very professional as they attended to Jordan. Milo and Carol stood together watching the experts work and didn't notice that the police had also arrived. Carol was trembling and crying as she hugged Milo. The head of the EMT crew asked for the victim's name and next of kin. Milo gave him the details and asked which hospital they would be using. The ambulance left quickly. The entire process took only a few minutes but, once again, Milo thought it took much longer.

Two police officers approached Carol, who was trying to gather her thoughts to answer the questions being asked. The officers took her statement since she was first on the scene, and said they would follow up with Jordan later at the hospital. As they turned to leave, one patrolman asked about Milo's relation to the victim. "She's my partner. May I go to the hospital now?" The officers said, "Yes." Milo told Carol to go home. "I'll call you with details later."

Carol asked if he locked the office. He didn't think so. She said, "I'll go do that, you go see to Jordan. Don't forget to call me." Milo picked up his blood-soaked keys and wiped them off as best he could on his shirt, he put Jordan's bloody purse in the trunk and a few seconds later was off to the hospital. The traffic wasn't cooperating, and it took over thirty minutes to arrive. He parked and moved as quickly as he could to the main desk in the lobby. He waited nervously in the short line before he could ask about Jordan. The nurse checked the computer. "Jordan Sutton is in surgery on the third floor." He turned and anxiously waited for the elevator which was now on the ninth floor, but descending. Finally, the elevator doors opened, Milo and several others entered. A lady selected 4 on the panel and asked Milo, "What floor?" "Three please."

The pleasant elevator voice announced, "Third floor." Milo rushed directly to the nurse's station. The young woman in charge looked up and smiled, "How may I help you?" Milo asked about Jordan. "Let me check. Are you a relative?" Milo, trying to act normal spoke quietly and showed her his business card. "Yes, I am." She scanned the computer screen. "Ms. Sutton is currently in surgery." She directed him to the waiting area across the lobby. "I'll let you know when she's moved to a room." Milo took a seat and called Carol. He gave her a hurried recap of what was going on and she could tell he was stressed. She told him to take a breath, and not to worry about the office. "Concentrate on Jordan. I forwarded the calls, so I can work from home. Everything will be fine." Milo was about to hang up when he remembered that Jordan was on her way to meet a new client. He mentioned the meeting to Carol who said she had the client's contact information and would call the lady. Milo logged on to his office computer from his cell phone and shut the system down. Then he tried to relax. He sat for a moment, got a cup of coffee from a service cart and called CR. He had to leave a message. Now, just like a stakeout, he had to sit and wait.

It was a few minutes past seven PM when a gentle voice asked, "Are you Mr. Starr?" He said yes, in a whispered voice so as not to wake the sleeping grandmother across the waiting room. The nurse explained that Jordan was awake and asking for him. He yawned as he followed the nurse to Jordan's curtained-off area of a wardroom. She was very groggy, but managed a smile. Milo was very relieved and couldn't resist kissing her on the forehead. "You smell like a hospital." Jordan smiled much broader. She whispered, "Well, what did you expect?" He smiled and asked, "Do you know what happened?"

She motioned for him to come close. "I ah…" She was a bit woozy and stopped talking. "I was in the parking garage and a guy asked if I was Jordan Sutton?" She stopped talking and dozed off. About five seconds later she continued. "…Are you Jordan Sutton? I turned around and saw a big guy with a gun. He was wearing a dark hoodie with red stripes on the sleeves and that's all I remember." She slipped away again as her medication started to take effect.

Milo touched her hand gently and turned to leave when she grabbed his arm. "I...I... saw the same guy at the steakhouse the other night, the other...night. He was...sitting at the bar." Milo leaned in to ask, "Are you sure?" She slowly nodded yes as she drifted away again. He continued to hold her hand in case she had more to say, but she was beginning to snore quietly. The nurse entered and checked Jordan's chart. "She's going to be asleep for the night." As he was leaving the room an incoherent Jordan asked, "Where's my purse?" Then she fell asleep again. "When she wakes, please tell her that I have her purse." The nurse smiled and made a note on her chart.

Milo returned to the waiting room and called Carol. He gave her a more concise version of the events of the day. "Jordan's asleep now. I think I should go home for a while, I have blood all over my clothes." Carol agreed, "Oh, by the way, I called the lady Jordan was going to meet and she said they didn't have a meeting scheduled. We'll talk tomorrow." Milo ended the call and realized that the phony meeting was a setup. He started toward the elevators but was stopped by the two police officers he met earlier in his parking garage. "Mr. Starr, can we talk?"

CHAPTER 30

Bad Day...
About to get Worse!

The two police officers moved their conversation away from the Nurses Station. They asked Milo if he had a business card and they wanted to hear his version of what happened to Ms. Sutton. Milo told them exactly what he saw in the parking garage and then relayed his recent conversation with Jordan before she fell asleep. "She said the shooter was a big guy who was wearing a dark hoodie with red stripes on the sleeves, who knew her name." One of the officers made a note. "She also said that she'd seen him before sitting at the bar of a restaurant we frequent." The officer asked, "When was that?" Milo was a bit scrambled but said, "I think that was night before last." The police officer made a note of that too.

"Did *you* see this guy at the restaurant?" "No, I was facing away from the bar. I would have thought it was a random event, if Jordan hadn't mentioned seeing him at the bar. I guess he was following us." The officer closed his notebook and looked at Milo's business card. "I know your name, sir. You've been in the news lately, because of some cases you solved." The other officer looked around and quietly said, "Maybe someone is pissed at you because you folks solve a lot of crimes." Milo thought that over. "That's possible, but since most of our dangerous cases are closed, I doubt it." The officers shook Milo's hand and thanked him for his statement, and told him to watch his back. They said they would contact him if they needed more information.

The officers walked towards the Information Desk and Milo pushed the down button. When he stepped into the elevator, he was thinking about the phony meeting with the mother. *"Maybe both of us were supposed to be in the garage."* The more he thought about everything that happened, the more upset he became. The elevator stopped at the second floor, then the main lobby. He was trying to make sense out of it all as the calming female elevator voice said, "first floor." The doors opened, and Milo stepped out into a small group waiting to enter the elevator. He pushed his way through the group and glanced across the main lobby where he thought he saw a large man sitting in the corner wearing a dark hoodie with red stripes on the sleeves. When he cleared himself from the waiting group, the man was gone.

Milo rescanned the lobby, then quickly turned away and exited the building. As he walked the long concrete pathway toward the parking garage he removed his weapon from the holster under his right armpit and placed it in his left jacket pocket. *"Just in case,"* he thought as he put his hand on the trigger. When he rounded the corner in the darkened parking structure, he heard a deep, raspy voice behind him ask, "Are you Milo Starr?"

That question triggered Milo's response as he remembered what Jordan just told him. The nimble P.I. immediately turned, dropped to his right knee and fired one shot from inside his jacket pocket, hitting the big man in the thigh. The would-be killer fired two shots that both missed their target and careened off the ceiling as he fell to the concrete floor. Milo was on an adrenalin rush as he moved to disarm the guy in the hoodie with red stripes on the sleeves. Milo moved closer and held him at gunpoint while he called CR. "I just shot a guy who tried to kill me, and I think he's the one who shot Jordan too." Milo gave CR his location and their FBI buddy told him to subdue the guy, "Someone will be there soon. "Do you have handcuffs with you?" "Yeah!" "Well, lock him up till my men get there."

Milo, still holding his gun, was barely able to get the cuffs on the bleeding suspect. It wasn't a textbook operation, but it worked. He cuffed him in front, so he could apply pressure to his wound and then dragged him up against the parking structure wall. The man was struggling as Milo pushed against his leg. There was a lot of blood, so Milo unbuckled his belt and wrapped it around the bleeding thigh. He realized he must have hit an artery so, he pulled the belt tighter. "Keep pressure on that or you'll bleed out right here before the cops arrive." The guy grunted. "Why are you trying to kill me and my partner?" The man said nothing. "Who put you up to this?"

Again, nothing but a groan. "Well, you're going to jail and if we can tie you to some Las Vegas murders, you'll be gone for a long time." The injured man tried not to show how much he was hurting when he talked. "I didn't have nothin' to do with anything in Vegas. I only work here in L.A." Milo put some pressure on the wound. "What's your name?" The suspect muttered, "Gino." Milo applied a little more pressure which made the suspect cringe. "Well Gino, before the authorities drag your ass away, I want to know who told you to shoot us and why." Gino struggled to answer and tried not to act as if he were hurt.

"The why is easy. It's because you're costin' somebody a lot of money!" Milo pushed on his thigh a little harder. "Who ordered it?" Gino groaned and looked deep into Milo's eyes, "If I give you that name, you might as well kill me now." Milo who was still on an adrenaline high, stepped back and raised his weapon. "How about Vegas? Do you know anything about what's going on there?" Gino muttered a simple, "No." Milo asked the bleeding suspect if he had a cell phone. Gino said, "Yeah, in my pocket." Milo searched the pockets of the hoodie and found the phone. "Well, whoever sent you isn't going to kill you, and neither am I. I'll leave that up to the state."

With a few clicks Milo paired Gino's phone to his. He captured the entire call list just as the FBI appeared. "You Milo Starr?" "Yes." "I'm agent Danton. CR said to pick up someone and book him for attempted murder." Milo handed the agent his business card. "His name is Gino something and he's all yours." Two of CR's guys lifted the tall heavy-set man to his feet. "He has a gunshot wound to the leg. Tell CR he's guilty of two counts of attempted murder. Both Jordan Sutton and I will testify against him, if necessary."

Gino glared at Milo as the officers moved him toward their SUV. Milo handed Gino's cell phone to agent Danton as he asked for his handcuffs back. One of the FBI agents put their cuffs on Gino and sat him in the back of the SUV. They handed the bloody cuffs to Milo. He then turned away as Gino asked, "Are these real FBI agents?" Milo nodded, yes. "If I give you the name of the guy who set this up will that help me?" Milo leaned close. "If you give me his location too, yes it will." Gino realized that he was in deep and could use some help. "All the information is in my phone. His name is Mr. Z. His office address is there too. Go ahead, take my phone. Just don't let him know that I told you, okay?" Milo assured him that he wouldn't mention how they found out. He asked Agent Danton to give the phone to CR. "Tell him to let the D.A. know that Gino has been very helpful, and I'll call him later about everything; also tell CR he owes me a belt." Milo watched the SUV drive away and breathed a sigh of relief.

The blood on Milo's pants was still a little wet. He checked the trunk, dumped the bloody cuffs and found a large plastic bag which he placed on the front seat. As he closed the car door he sat for a moment and realized that this crazy case might be wrapped up soon. He put on his favorite jazz station and headed home. Once there, a very tired and stressed out Milo Starr showered, shaved and changed into an outfit that didn't have blood spatters all over it. He called the hospital and was told that Jordan was still sleeping and doing extremely well. She would probably be released late tomorrow or early the day after. He gave the nurse his cell number just in case. "If she wakes up, tell her I'll be over in the morning." He locked the condo and walked down the street to his new favorite bar, thinking all the while that there was something else he was supposed to do. He was too frazzled to come up with the answer.

Ten minutes later he was seated and ordering a Margarita with salt at Jordan's Steakhouse. He kept thinking about the peanuts at Margo-Rita's. "*If this bar had that feature, then I'd really be set.*" While he waited, he received a text from CR. ***"Booked the guy you shot, got his phone. Now what?"*** Milo took a deep breath and finally remembered what he was supposed to do. He opened Gino's phone and searched the information he cloned. Scanning the call log, he found a listing for Mr. Z with his address. He placed a call to CR and had to leave a message. "Call me back ASAP."

He watched the bartender concoct his drink with salt and a slice of lime. It looked frosty-good and tasted even better. He complimented the bartender and introduced himself. "I've seen you here a few times. Thanks for coming back. I'm Jerry. Glad you like the drink." Milo sat sipping and thinking about the events of the day. His phone vibrated, it was CR calling. Milo gave him a fast rundown of his day. CR asked about Jordan and wanted to know why Agent Danton gave him a phone. "First, Jordan will be fine, thanks for asking. Here's the deal about the phone."

Milo took a small sip of his drink. "The guy I shot is named Gino something. He shot Jordan twice and tried to get me, but I put one in his leg. You with me so far?" CR said he understood and Milo continued. "After Gino was cuffed he said he didn't have anything to do with Vegas. He only works here in L.A. The guy who ordered the hit on me and Jordan is definitely involved in everything. He told Gino that we cost him a crap-load of money in Vegas." CR asked if he had the name of the man who ordered the hit. "Yes, it's in Gino's phone. Look in his contact list for a Mr. Z, as in zebra. That's the guy behind all of this. His address is there too."

CR wanted to record this conversation, so he asked Milo the questions again. "*Agent CR Reid speaking with Milo Starr. Please give me all the information you have.*" Milo went through the events of the day and gave CR the complete rundown again. "CR, that's about it. Except, when your guys arrest Mr. Z, tell them to put the cuffs on extra tight." CR said he'd try to make that happen. He was happy that Jordan was going to be okay. Milo's second drink arrived. "CR, I found some notes on a remote server that indicate that this project would be expanding soon. They are attempting to set up this credit card scam at a bunch of other hotels in high-tourist areas." CR laughed, "But, little-old-you and Jordan stopped them. No wonder somebody wants your head on a stick." Milo raised his glass, "Thanks, old friend for that wonderful image. We owe you dinner as soon as Jordan is given the all-clear." "I look forward to it. Give her my best. We'll talk soon."

Milo finished his second drink and made sure he cleaned all the salt from the rim of the glass. Jerry saw he was empty and wanted to know if he could stand another. "How about a flavored Margarita?" Jerry suggested either strawberry or guava. Milo selected the latter without salt this time. He started his things to do list on a napkin. The list read: Call Carol - pick up flowers - see Jordan and then he added, EXPANSION! He said, "That's why they needed the scanner, it was a sample, a prototype so they could have more made for the expansion." Then he realized that he was talking loudly to himself, there was no Jordan.

He finished the list, put it in his pocket and tasted the new drink which was fantastic. He was feeling terrific and then his phone rang. He looked at the caller ID and saw it wasn't a number he recognized. The screen displayed **FWD from** and it listed another number. Then it hit him, he was getting Gino's calls because he cloned his phone. Milo waited and after three rings voicemail cut in. He listened to the message. A man with a deep voice said, *"Gino, I just learned that the broad is still alive in a hospital on the west side. Finish that job and take care of Starr too, or it's your ass on the line."* He called CR and told him about the message. "You can listen because it's on Gino's phone too. When are you moving on Mr. Z?" "Very soon. We have his office and home address and we'll be working both scenes at the same time. I'll call you if we have him." Milo sat finishing his new favorite drink at his new favorite bar.

He wandered over to the hostess and asked for a table. She seated him and his drink. Mr. Jordan stopped by the table. "Dining alone?" "Yes, my partner had an appointment." Mr. Jordan recommended the special of the day, a broiled pork chop. Milo thought that was an excellent suggestion. When his salad arrived, he realized that he hadn't eaten anything all day and was very hungry. The background piano music really helped calm him down, but as he looked across the table at the empty chair, he became anxious again. He hoped Jordan would return unscathed by this experience and would be back with him soon.

The stuffed pork chop and salad were perfect. His waiter approached and asked, "Dessert?" Milo's brain was telling him he deserved it. "Yes, I'll have the cheesecake and coffee please." He received a text from CR.

We got him! Mr. Z is in custody. Singing like a bird. We have the full story. He was only one cog in this scheme. He made a deal and named a bunch of people in Vegas and at hotels in Chicago, NYC and Dallas. Seems they were ready to branch out. We contacted local agencies and they plan to arrest all of them, soon. Thanks again.

Milo smiled and couldn't wait to tell Jordan about the events of the day. He sat drinking his coffee and listening to the piano music. It was a nice way to end the day except for the empty chair across from him. Milo smiled and felt great about their work on this case. He placed a call to James Forbes and had to leave a message. *James, this is Milo. Looks like we've caught the people running the scam. Call me.* He finished the cheesecake which was wonderful. The happy P.I. put a twenty in the tip jar on the piano, said goodnight to Mr. Jordan and Jerry at the bar and took a leisurely stroll up the street to his condo. Once inside, he charged his phone, set the perimeter alarm and got ready for bed. He had a strange feeling tonight. He used to love living alone, but not anymore. An empty house is a lonely house.

CHAPTER 31

Tomorrow, Tomorrow

Milo didn't sleep too well. He tossed and turned and kept waking up at all hours. The restlessness wasn't work-related; he was really worried about Jordan. He finally gave up trying to sleep and started his morning ritual as the sun began to rise. Coffee was always the first order of business. With that task completed, he sat on their small balcony and watched the morning slowly appear. He was still trying to wake up when the hospital called to say that Jordan would be staying one more day. The pleasant-sounding nurse gave him a short update on her condition and then said, "Ms. Sutton wants to leave now, but her doctor feels it would be best if she stays another day. She should be ready to leave tomorrow about noon." Milo thanked the nurse and asked her to tell Jordan that he would be over this morning to see her.

James called, and Milo gave him a play-by-play description of the shootings and arrests. "It's not one-hundred percent finished, but we're close." James said he was going to a hotel owners' meeting soon. "I'll ask how many are having trouble with over-charging. Please tell Jordan to take care." Milo assured James that he would.

After a second coffee, it was time to begin the day. He was in the middle of shaving when Carol called. He hit the speaker button and kept talking while he shaved. She wanted to know when Jordan was getting out of the hospital. "I was just wondering if I should go over and see her." Milo told their resident mother hen that he was going there about eleven. "She'll be released tomorrow." Carol said she'd see him at the hospital. He finished shaving, dressed quickly and decided to head out early to complete his things to do list. After a quick breakfast, he picked up some flowers for his favorite lady and partner.

Jordan was all smiles when Milo and Carol arrived each with giant bouquets of flowers. "When am I getting out of here?" "Not until tomorrow, so just relax, smell the flowers and enjoy your Jell-O." Carol wanted to know all about what happened. Jordan was a bit hazy on the details. She squeezed Milo's hand. "Do you know what happened? I really can't remember everything." He closed the door and motioned for Carol to come closer to the bed, so he could speak softly. He started with the shooting at their office parking garage. "Remember you were walking to the car when a guy asked you if you were Jordan Sutton?" She nodded but wasn't a hundred percent sure. "Yeah, I vaguely remember that. He was big and was wearing something with red stripes." Milo smiled and quickly continued. "Yeah, a hoodie with red stripes on the sleeves. That's the guy that shot you twice; Carol found you and here you are." Carol added, "I never saw that much blood, I thought you were, well you know."

Milo continued regaling them with his adventure in the hospital's parking structure. "I left your room and thought I saw the guy in the hoodie sitting in the lobby. I walked quickly to my car inside the parking structure. On the way, I put my revolver in my coat pocket, just in case. I heard someone behind me ask if I was Milo Starr and thanks to what you told me, I went into action." He stepped away from her bed and demonstrated what he did by dropping to one knee. "I shot him in the leg from inside my coat pocket. Great shot, huh?" Jordan leaned over to Carol. "I think he's adding a few details for dramatic effect." Milo laughed. "No, I didn't add anything, that's what really happened. Look, here's the hole in my jacket." Jordan smirked at Carol. "He could have caught that on a nail." Milo shook his head as he said, "If you test my coat you'll find gunshot residue." Jordan decided to mess with him some more. "He probably fired his pistol by accident."

Milo was getting a little annoyed as he continued. "It all happened just the way I said it happened. Anyway, the name of the guy who shot you is Gino and here comes the best part."

He described how he cloned Gino's phone and then how the FBI caught the guy who was behind the Las Vegas murders and credit card scam. "The guy behind everything is a Mr. Z as in zebra, and he's in custody right now." Milo stopped and was expecting a round of applause, but that didn't happen. Jordan looked at Carol. "Mr. Z? You want us to believe that you caught a mastermind named Mr. Z? Is he a superhero?" Milo started laughing because even he realized how improbable the story sounded.

"OK, you don't have to believe me, but CR did. He not only believed me, but he arrested Mr. Z, and the FBI plans to arrest a bunch of people connected to the credit card scam in Las Vegas, Chicago, Dallas and a few other locations. They were getting ready to expand in many other cities. The case is almost totally wrapped up." Jordan squeezed his hand, "I'm glad you weren't hit." Milo gently squeezed back, "No, I'm fine. It's all over but the shouting." He smiled and waited for applause. Once again, there wasn't any.

Jordan sat back in bed. "Wow, all that took place while I was flat on my back. I should get shot more often." She laughed but stopped because it really hurt to laugh. Carol didn't think that was funny at all. She glared at Jordan, "Don't even joke about that." Carol told them that the answering service was full of messages, but they would keep until tomorrow. "You just rest and get better." Milo suddenly remembered, "You mentioned the answering service, listen to this." He fumbled with his phone and was able to recall the voice mail message on Gino's phone. "Okay, what you're about to hear came in last night. It's a message to Gino, the guy who shot you, from the mysterious Mr. Z." The ladies listened and were finally convinced that Milo was telling the truth.

Jordan smiled as she looked at Carol. "Well, I guess the other P.I. in the room wasn't just making up a story. That makes me feel better. I'll be out of here tomorrow, I'm tough you know." Milo took her hand,

"But soft to the touch." They both sat with Jordan joking and talking until visiting hours where over. Jordan was relieved that the Vegas case was coming to an end. "Did you call James and Kate?" Milo kissed her on the forehead, "You asked me that before. Yes, I called them and gave them the full story. They wished you a speedy recovery. I'll see you early tomorrow. Rest." Carol hugged her. "Take care of yourself." Then she turned to Milo. "I'm hungry. You're buying?" Milo took Carol's arm. "Yes, I'll take you to our new favorite steakhouse." Jordan thought that was a great idea and said, "You can take me there tomorrow night." Milo looked at his lovely partner and told her to take it easy and eat her Jell-O. Milo smiled and waved as he and Carol headed out. Jordan turned on the TV to watch the news and relax.

Carol followed Milo into the parking lot of the steakhouse. She parked and laughed when she saw the Jordan's Steakhouse sign. "That's funny." Milo told her they really enjoy the food, the service and the bar. The owner saw Milo and welcomed him and his guest. Carol looked around and told Mr. Jordan how much she loved the fashionable décor. "I'm glad you like the look, I hope you enjoy the food as much, if not more." They sat, ordered and had a great time talking away the early evening. Carol called her husband to tell him she would be home soon. Milo suggested that she take home a dinner for him. "Good idea." Milo called the waiter over and told Carol to place a to-go order. She told the waiter, "Make it the same as mine, a filet, medium." The waiter thought that was an excellent choice.

Milo told her that Jordan would probably stay home to rest for a few days. "Do we have a lot of calls and things to catch up on?" "Yes, you have a pile of things to look over."

"Okay, tomorrow, after I pick her up, I'll be in." He and Carol, with her "to-go order" said goodnight to Mr. Jordan. Milo helped Carol into her car. "See you tomorrow afternoon, I guess." He watched her drive away and started toward his car then stopped. He thought, "*Do I really want to go home?*" Realizing that it was way too quiet at the condo without Jordan, he went back inside his new favorite bar and noticed that they would be open for another three hours.

He ordered a drink and called the hospital. The nurse checked and said, "She's sleeping." "Is she being released tomorrow?" "Yes, at noon." Milo ended the call and relaxed at the bar listening to soft piano music in the background. His phone interrupted his downtime.

It was James Forbes. "Milo, our phones have been down all day. Do you have any updates for us?" "Maybe I do. I don't remember how much I told you. It's been a crazy day." James said they also had a crazy day, "Just start at the beginning and tell us everything. I'll put you on speaker, so Kate can hear too." Milo told them about Jordan's shooting, Gino, the arrests. "The case is about ninety-nine percent wrapped up. Tell Charlie to dump all the scanners in the trash."

James wanted Milo to know about what happened at the latest hotel association meeting. "I asked if anybody was having trouble with a lot of credit card over-charging and five owners said yes." Milo told him to call those owners and tell them they should dump all the scanners too. "Tell them what we did with your staff and let them know they should do the same, and make sure they know there will be no repercussions. The scam is over. We caught the people who were running the operation. They're in custody and talking." They both agreed that all the hotels were going to have to fire and hire a lot of people. Milo added, "And make sure they do deep background checks on anyone they hire from now on." Kate laughed, "Maybe we should have you and Jordan do the vetting. Please give her our best and thank her for everything. Let's talk more when she's back home." Milo thanked them for the thought and assured them that she'd be back to work soon. "Have her call us as soon as she's out of the hospital." Milo said he'd make sure they talked with her.

It was noon and Milo arrived on time to collect his partner, who according to the nursing staff, had been ready to leave since dawn. He settled her account and followed the nurse, pushing a wheelchair to Jordan's room. The injured P.I. was very anxious to leave. When she saw Milo, she brightened up even more. "It's about time," she said with a smile. "Sorry I'm late, I was out to breakfast with my girlfriend." She started to hit him with her left hand and stopped because it was in a sling. Instead, she smacked him with her right hand. "Let's go." The nurse told him to bring the car around and they would meet him at the front door. Milo was all smiles as he went to get the car. On the way to the parking lot he flashed back to the last time he made this same walk. He didn't see any evidence of what happened there. He thought *"Was that just the day before yesterday?"* He remembered that Gino had fired twice, and the bullets missed him. He glanced at the walls and then noticed the ceiling had two small chunks of concrete missing. He started the car thinking, *"I was very lucky."*

He thanked the nurse and helped Jordan into the car. "Make sure she gets plenty of rest, and takes her pills." Milo told the charming young lady he'd get Jordan to do everything she is supposed to do. The patient was very quiet. "How do you feel?" She smiled at him. "I'm fine. This isn't the first time I've been shot, you know. I'll heal fast." Milo drove away from the hospital and turned toward the condo. "Aren't we going to the office?" "No, you're going to bed." She squinted her eyes and looked at him. "No, we have phone calls to return and appointments to make." Milo explained that Carol had contacted all the new clients and she set up appointments for next week. "We're going home and you're going to bed." She smiled, "Great, we're going to bed." Milo laughed at her as he pulled into their parking spot. "No, **we're** not going to bed; you're going to bed all by yourself."

He helped her into the condo, tucked her in and arranged the pill bottles on the nightstand. He read the labels and made a quick chart to make sure she took her meds on time. He called Carol and told her what was up. "Sure, you can talk to her." He handed the phone to Jordan. The ladies chatted for about twenty minutes. "I don't know, I'll ask. Milo, when are we going to the office?" He couldn't believe the question. "Tell her, I'll be there in the morning."

Jordan smiled and told Carol, "We'll both be there tomorrow. Bye." Milo sat next to her on the bed. "You're not going anywhere, you have to rest." Jordan told him that she could rest on his office couch, "It's very comfortable. I won't make calls or bother you or anything." She sounded so cute that Milo had to give in. "Alright, but you don't move a muscle." Jordan smiled and closed her eyes.

During the evening, Milo made sure that Jordan took her pills. She seemed to be doing well. He re-heated some Chinese food for dinner and she ate a little and then was sleeping so peacefully he didn't want to disturb her. He sacked out on the living room couch and as usual, morning came too quickly. He was awakened by the sound of the coffee grinder.

"What are you doing?" She mumbled something, but he couldn't understand her. Milo joined her in the kitchen. "Are you okay?" She, very matter-of-factly said, "Yeah, I'm fine, how are you?" She continued to make the coffee and acted as if she had never been shot. Milo didn't understand it, but he accepted her attitude. She handed him a cup of hot morning cheer and motioned for him to join her on their small balcony. "So, you've been busy, haven't you?" He laughed, "Yes, I have." He then went over the story again. He told her about CR, the FBI arrests and Mr. Z. "So, there really is a Mr. Z. I didn't dream all that?"

Milo laughed again, "No, you didn't dream it. I know it sounds like a comic book name, but it happened just the way I said it did, and the case is almost wrapped up. I talked with CR and he thinks they finally understand the full concept behind everything." Jordan wanted to hear it all. "Mr. Z was operating in Vegas as a test-run. Next month, they were going to expand to hotels in Miami, Chicago, Dallas and a bunch of other tourist cities. That's about it. Looks like CR and the cops have arrested almost everybody involved." Jordan finished her coffee, put her cup in the sink and announced, "I'm gonna get dressed for the office." She stooped and turned. "I guess I could use some assistance getting dressed."

Milo helped her, but couldn't believe she wanted to go the office. "You sure you feel okay?" As she went to the bathroom she said, "I'm fine, please put all my pills and the schedule you made, in a bag." Milo did as he was told and then got dressed for work. He tried to help Jordan into the car, but she got in on her own. She only needed him to secure her seat belt.

CHAPTER 32

More Publicity

Carol was overjoyed to see them and lightly hugged Jordan. "You had me worried." Jordan told her about today's deal. "I'm not supposed to do anything but rest." Milo escorted their patient to the couch. Milo told Jordan to do nothing. "I can make phone calls, can't I?" Carol looked at Milo for his approval. He gave up and nodded yes. Carol retrieved their call lists. "Here they are, now get to work. But Jordan, don't move. Just ask me if you need anything." Carol started to leave. "Sorry you got shot, but I'm glad you're here and gonna be fine." Jordan thanked her for her concern. "I'll be back to normal, soon." Carol went into the lobby leaving S & S to make new client calls.

They worked on the phones all day. Jordan finished her call list and looked at Milo. "I have nine new appointments for next week. I set them for Wednesday, Thursday and Friday." Milo said he wasn't that lucky, he only got two. "I also set them for next week. Tuesday and Wednesday. Look at the time, where did the day go? It's getting dark already. Let's go eat." As Milo started to straighten up his desk he received a text message from CR. ***The Vegas papers got hold of the story about the credit card scam. - It's being run here and in L.A. too with your names.*** Milo showed Jordan the text. "Well, here we go again." She thought it was gonna be great publicity for them. "I'm sure we'll have a ton of calls tomorrow." As she headed toward the lobby, the phone rang. Carol answered and put them on hold.

"It's the L.A. Times wanting to do a follow-up story on the Vegas case you solved." Milo said, "It's getting late. Tell them we'll call them in the morning." When she hung up, there were more calls lighting up her phone. Over the next thirty-minutes Carol fielded all of them giving everyone the same answer. She went back to Milo's office. "You're gonna have a busy day tomorrow. In addition to the Times, calls came in from CBS, NBC, ABC, Fox and several Internet News Services. They all want to talk with both of you. I told everybody we'd call them back early tomorrow. Should I leave for the day?" Jordan said, "Sure, let the service pick up any other calls." Milo agreed, "See you in the morning."

As she was leaving, Carol took one more call. She put them on hold. "It's a TV news service, the one that distributes to all of the major networks. They have a crew very close to us and would like to send them over now." She waited for an answer. "They said it would be a quick shoot, but it would be easier than giving twenty interviews." Jordan yelled, "Oh…I look like crap. Do they have to do it now?" "They said the crew is close by and it won't take long. They want to get it on the late news here and Las Vegas." Milo looked at his lovely partner, "It's up to you. You look fine to me." Jordan made a face. "Fine isn't good enough."

Jordan mumbled, "Okay, tell them yes." She looked at Milo and told him, "Fix your hair and tie." Milo wasted no time in doing a quick fix-up. Jordan yelled to Carol, "Please bring in the Beautee Plus Cosmetics and a comb and mirror." All three of them spruced up and were looking good by the time the news crew arrived. They quickly set up the camera and two small lights in Milo's office. The reporter pulled up a chair next to the camera and began to fire questions about their involvement in the wrap-up of the massive credit card fraud scam in Las Vegas. Milo wasn't sure how much they should say about the arrests. "We worked on this case for quite a while and were able to bring the scam, as you call it, to an end. The masterminds behind these crimes put out a hit on us because we were costing them millions. They shot Jordan twice and the FBI took them into custody."

The camera zoomed in on Jordan and the reporter asked about her injuries. The reporter mentioned that they were told multiple hotels were involved. Jordan said, "Yes, that's true, but we've pulled the plug on the entire operation." Milo jumped in to say, "Since it's an on-going investigation, we can't give you more details at this time."

Then the reporter asked Milo what special enlightenment helped them solve this million-dollar fraud. Milo paused, smiled and reverted to his stock answer. "Once again, we used deductive reasoning and the help of the FBI and local law enforcement." The reporter ended by saying, "That's the same answer you gave us when you solved the mutilation murders." Milo smiled, took Jordan's hand and brought the interview to an end by saying, "That's how Sutton and Starr do everything."

The camera operator and reporter thanked them and said, "This interview will run on the late news if we get out of here right now. Once everything is wrapped up on this case, can we do a follow-up interview?" Milo and Jordan of course agreed. The reporter and two-man crew packed and left quickly. When the door closed, Milo looked at Jordan and Carol. "You guys ready to leave?" Carol told them, "Yes, let's get out of here before USA Today shows up. See both of you tomorrow." Carol put the phone on the service and closed the front door.

Jordan was feeling better than she should, considering what she had been through. "I want to go out to eat." Milo turned off his desk light and helped her off the couch. "Great, where to?" She smiled, "The same place you took Carol, Jordan's Steakhouse." Milo agreed as he set the alarm system and locked the office.

On the way to the car CR called. "Hi, FBI guy, what's up?" He wanted to know where they were right now. "We're about to head to dinner at Jordan's Steakhouse, down the block from our condo, why?" "I'll tell you in person, I'll meet you there." "Ok, we'll see you soon." They entered the car and headed out to the steakhouse. "CR is going to meet us at the restaurant. "Why?" Milo didn't know. "We'll find out when we get there."

CHAPTER 33

Time to Calm Down

As they entered the steakhouse, the very attentive owner came over to welcome them back and noticed Jordan's sling. "Sorry to see you've had some trouble." He quietly told her, "If you order a steak, I'll make sure the chef slices it for you." Jordan smiled, "Thank you for the great service." He showed them to their table. "We're expecting someone to join us." Mr. Jordan told them he'd bring their guest over. Their waiter asked if they wanted something from the bar. Milo ordered a gin and tonic with lime, "But no drinking for you, young lady." She smiled, "I know. I'll have iced tea, please." She touched Milo's hand, "But thanks for calling me young."

Milo toasted his partner with a water glass, "You are one tough, yet soft lady. Have I told you how much I love you?" Jordan's tea arrived, and she raised her glass to Milo and flashed her promise ring. "Thank you for the compliment and no, you haven't told me that today." "Well, I do." They touched glasses just as CR showed up. Milo stood and motioned to the well-dressed FBI agent to join them. CR leaned down to hug

Jordan. "Glad you're up and about." She acted like miss tough gal, "I'm gonna be fine, I've been shot before." Milo laughed, "She talks a good game. Please, join us." CR sat and drank some of Milo's ice water. "Why did you want to see us?"

CR said he was hungry. "I just wanted to meet you, and have you buy me a fancy dinner." Milo laughed, raised his drink and exclaimed, "You're right, we *do* owe you a fancy dinner and a big thank you." Jordan thought it was nice of him to mention them at the two press conferences in connection to the mutilation murders. CR looked up from his menu. "Did you get a lot of responses from the press conferences?" "Yes, from prospective clients and a lot of news coverage and we received a nice check from the city." Jordan added, "That's why James and Kate Forbes' called us to help them in Las Vegas. They read about us solving the murder case." Jordan told him about the quickie interview they did just a little while ago. "They asked about the Las Vegas case. It's airing tonight on the late news."

CR smiled. "I'm glad I could help you. After all the help you gave the FBI, you deserved the recognition. That's why I'm here, but let's order first." Milo said that the filet was always excellent. They all ordered filets with sides of vegetables. Jordan was about to mention what the owner said they would do for her when their very attentive waiter smiled, nodded and showed Jordan his order pad which already had this note. *"Please cut steak, small pieces for customer."* She smiled as Milo looked at CR. "Alright, we've ordered. Now, drop the other shoe, why are you here?"

CR looked at his ex-college chums and smiled. "Remember a while ago when I said the FBI needed your help on the mutilation case?" They both nodded. "Well, the powers that be finally agreed that you both went above and beyond the call of duty." He turned to Milo. "Everyone is very excited that you were able to solve those murders and now, you both bring down Mr. Z, whose real name is Zacharias, and his massive organization." He raised his water glass, "Congratulations. Just sorry you got hurt in the process. Maybe on the next case, Milo gets his butt kicked." Jordan smiled and raised her iced tea to CR.

Everyone watched as the plate of appetizers arrived, and CR eagerly dug-in, taking a bacon-wrapped mushroom from the platter. He began to tell them as much as he could remember as he munched. "Mr. Z had been planning this scam for a long time. He implemented everything over a two-year period and was almost ready to expand the operation to several other tourist destinations. We think they took each of the six Vegas hotels for several million bucks, maybe more." Milo asked, "How many others were involved? I figured Mr. Z wasn't working alone." CR continued, "He implicated people in three other cities and gave up the names of six General Managers in Las Vegas. He's the one who ordered the hits on you and the general managers also." Milo raised his drink to CR. "With all that against him he'll be behind bars for a long time." Jordan smiled, "I'm glad you got it all wrapped up." CR tipped his water glass to both of them. "Not one-hundred percent, but close."

Milo and Jordan were happy the case was almost over, and she asked, "What did Erin say when you told her about the big-time Vegas wedding?" CR looked down at the table and muttered. "I didn't mention it, yet." Jordan suddenly wasn't smiling anymore. She glared at him. "What the hell are you waiting for? You have to tell her!" CR said he would get around to it. Jordan shook her finger in his face. "You better, because it's going to be a beautiful affair." Their long-time friend promised, "Okay, I will. I've been so busy. I haven't been able to see her in over a week." Then he attempted to change the subject.

"I have something that will put a smile on your faces right now." He reached in his inside pocket and put an envelope on the table in front of Jordan. "The bureau wanted me to make sure you got the correct amount for your work on the city-wide case. I checked the hours and found I had made a mistake." Jordan didn't understand. "You already gave us a big check. Do you want it back?" CR smiled and assured them they could keep what they were given. "This is a smaller check for some additional hours I found."

Their dinners arrived, and Jordan thanked their waiter for her pre-sliced steak. Milo explained that unlike some Investigators, they don't keep track of the hours they spend on cases. "So, we really have no idea." CR smiled, "Well, you're in luck because as I mentioned to you before, I make notes about every meeting and phone call I have. Take a look." The one-armed lady put down her fork and handed the envelope to Milo who opened it and removed the check.

Milo looked at the amount and tried not to smile. He showed the check to Jordan who couldn't believe what she was seeing. "Wow, this is ours too?" CR replied, "It should have been included in the first payment, but I couldn't find all my notes." Milo raised his glass to CR. "Thank you for finding your notes and thank your bosses for the extra, nineteen-thousand dollars." Jordan was very happy about the payment. "Do you need anything from us?" CR removed another envelope from his coat and opened a folded piece of paper. "Just sign on the line indicating that you received the check. That's all." Milo signed and put the check in his coat pocket. CR said, "Thanks for your help. We might have solved that case ourselves, but it would have taken us a lot longer. Still not going to tell me how you did it?"

Jordan put down her fork. "He didn't even tell *me* how he did it." Milo smiled, "I've never said how we do anything because nobody would believe the answers." CR asked if it was that weird?" "Yes, weird enough." CR leaned over to Jordan and whispered, "Make him tell you." Dinner was once again, wonderful. They thanked CR for the check. He thanked them for dinner and the great work. Jordan hugged their old friend, "I think we owe you another dinner too.' "Fine with me, I'll see you guys soon." Jordan told him, "Next time you have to bring your fiancé, after you tell her about your Las Vegas surprise." CR agreed and waved as he left. Milo helped Jordan to the car and noticed that she seemed tired and might be ready for bed.

Once inside the condo, Jordan went to the bedroom while Milo charged his cell phone and activated their alarm system. He looked at her, sat on her side of the bed and asked, "How are you feeling?" She kissed him tenderly, "I'm just a little tired but I feel fine about our life. We're busy, we're making money, and I'm in love. What could be better?" Milo looked at her and jokingly said, "That depends. Who are you in love with?" She pushed him off the bed with her good arm and pulled back the top sheet on his side of the bed.

Milo said, "Don't go anywhere," as he headed to the shower. He was super-fast, but not fast enough because when he returned, Jordan's eyelids were drooping. He slipped into bed quietly and suddenly his beautiful sidekick forced her eyes to open. "Okay, show me some of that deductive reasoning." Milo laughed, turned off the lights and kissed the love of his life as she snuggled up to him. A few moments later, Jordan fell asleep in Milo's arms and that made for the perfect ending to a very bad week.

CHAPTER 34

The Honor
of Your Presence

With all the publicity Sutton & Starr received, their caseload was over the top. They had to spilt forces and flip coins to see who would take which case. Jordan worked her list in between visits to the physical therapist and occasionally, they combined forces and solved things together, but those times were few and far between. Their business suddenly became one of those *"be careful what you wish for prophecies."* They almost didn't have time for themselves or each other.

After weeks and weeks of non-stop, burn the midnight oil work, they both found themselves sitting quietly in the office. Milo checked his desk calendar, "I have no appointments today, what about you?" Jordan smiled and suddenly realized that she was also free. "Carol, do we have any appointments or meetings?" Carol entered Milo's office. "No, all quiet on the Private Investigator front. Strange huh?"

Milo's computer dinged. "Hold that thought, we might have a new case." He opened the email and looked at the ladies with a gigantic grin on his face.

"Guess who just told his fiancé about their dream wedding in Las Vegas?" Carol joked, "Well it's not you, so?" Jordan smiled and said, "Whoopee, CR finally did it." Milo kept reading the email. "He wants us to meet them for drinks. I'll say congratulations and yes to the drinks." Milo typed and sent the email. Carol left saying, "Does that give anybody else ideas?" Both Milo and Jordan shook their heads and yelled, "No!" Carol closed Milo's door with a slight bang.

Jordan asked, "What should we get them as a wedding gift?" Milo started to pace and suddenly stopped because he had a bright idea. "Remember we discussed giving CR a bonus for his help? But we decided we couldn't do that." Jordan nodded. Milo smiled and continued, "So, what if we give them a honeymoon somewhere?" Jordan thought that was a terrific idea. "There are a lot of wonderful resorts all over. Good thinking, young man but how can we figure out where they want to go?" Milo had no idea. Jordan walked slowly toward Milo's desk and turned his swivel chair to the side. She took a seat in his lap and kissed him. "I missed you." He caught his breath and quietly whispered, "I missed you too. Where you been?" Jordan pulled away slightly, "Working my butt off." Milo hugged her. "Just kidding. This is nice." She stood and walked to Carol's desk and said loudly, "How about we all take a proper vacation?" Nobody answered her.

That's when the wedding gift idea hit her. "I know what to give CR. Carol, could we send him and his bride on a honeymoon anywhere they choose? Is that possible?" Carol didn't know for sure but said she'd check with their travel agency. "It would be like an open account that would be charged to Milo once they decide." Carol made a note and said she'd check on it. Jordan looked into Milo's office. "How do you like that idea? The wedding couple gets to pick their own destination." Milo was about to answer when his computer beeped again. "Hold that thought. Let me see what this is. What's this?" He looked at his email and his mood changed. "It's from James and Kate. They are in Las Vegas to attend their General Manager's funeral. They said they heard from CR and have been working with him to pull the wedding together. He wants us to fly up with them for the occasion and wonders if we want to invite anybody." Milo looked at Jordan. "Carol?" Jordan smiled, "For sure. Oh, Carol, come in for a moment." She dropped everything and popped in fast. "What's up?"

Jordan asked if she could get a sitter for her kids and the cat for a few days. Carol looked around not knowing what to answer. "If it's to paint this place, the answer is no. But for anything else, maybe." Milo said, "Well we were going to ask you to paint." Jordan pretended to smack him on the arm. "No, we weren't. You know him, he's full of crap. Would you and your husband like to join us at CR's wedding in Las Vegas?" Carol was shocked. "Really?" They both said, "Yes, really."

Milo told her they would be flying with James and Kate Forbes and would be staying at their hotel. Carol leaned over to Milo. "I'm saying yes. Even if I have to give my kids and cat away, I'll be there. Just tell me when and what to wear." Milo made a note on his desk calendar to tell James and Kate about their guests.

"Jordan, I like your idea for the wedding gift. They can go anywhere they like." Jordan laughed, "What if they choose a private island somewhere?" He shook his head no. "They won't do that because there wouldn't be a super-fancy hotel with room service and a mini-bar. Have Carol contact the travel agency and see if it's possible." The office phone rang Milo picked up as Jordan went into the lobby area to talk to Carol about the trip.

"Yes, this is Milo Starr." He finished the conversation and Jordan wondered if they had a new client. "No, it was Charlie from the Golden Oasis. He heard from several hotels who asked about the scanners." Jordan sat on the edge of the desk. "What did you tell him?" "I told him to call all the hotels and tell them to remove the scanners and donate them to a local electronic waste collection. At least that way, the scanners will be helping some non-profit organization. I also told him that we'd be up there soon for a wedding."

TWO WEEKS LATER

Carol was very excited about meeting James and Kate Forbes and flying in their private plane. The hotel and the mini-suite where she and her hubby would be staying for two days, was way beyond her wildest dreams. She, like Jordan, over-packed a little. But Carol figured she wanted to look nice all the time and was prodding her husband to get off his big behind and get dressed for dinner. "Jordan and Milo invited us, and I want to play a few slot machines before food."

Dinner was very elegant. James and Kate were happy that everyone could make time to be there. There were several toasts to the wedding couple, Erin and CR. The couple thanked everyone for celebrating their special time. Following dinner, Kate presented everyone with tickets to see their Magic Spectacular in the Oasis Theatre. As they scattered for the theatre James grabbed Milo's arm. "We'd like you and Jordan to join us at ten tomorrow morning in Conference Room A." Milo looked confused. "I'll explain why, tomorrow." Milo took Jordan's arm and headed toward the theatre. "James wants to see us at ten tomorrow."

The magic show was great. It was a wonderful way to relieve the stress of the weeks of hard work. Following the program Kate took Jordan, Carol and Erin to the wedding chapel. It wasn't open, but Mrs. Forbes had the key. She switched on the subtle lighting and they took a stroll down the beautiful central hallway. They passed several small chapels and stopped at the end of the hall. "Erin, we're going to have your wedding in here, in our Orchid Chapel, if you approve. It's our most elegant setting. James and I were married here. It was a wonderful day." They entered, and all agreed that this was the perfect location for a wedding. Kate told Erin that she should imagine the chapel with flowers, music and their friends filling the room. Erin smiled, "It's going to be beautiful. I can't wait."

The ladies met up with their male counterparts in the lobby and each couple began to wander around the casino. Jordan said, "I'm hitting the Keno lounge." She hugged Milo and whispered, "You go play some expensive slots and win us lots of money." He told her he'd pick her up for bed in about an hour. She made a face. "Alright, if I have to." The night went well and both Jordan and Milo left the casino "winners."

WEDDING DAY

After a wonderful breakfast buffet, Sutton and Starr took the elevators to the third floor. They entered Conference Room A and were surprised by a room full of people sitting around a large conference table. Milo was about to apologize for interrupting their meeting when James said, "Good morning, Milo. Come on in, you're in the right place." James looked at the seated group and announced, "This is Milo Starr and Jordan Sutton."

Everyone in the conference room stood and broke into a loud round of applause. S & S stopped and looked around the room, but didn't know what was going on. James smiled at the P.I. duo. "Milo, Jordan, you've helped everyone in this room and they just want to say thank you." Kate smiled and stepped between the pair and took their arms. "These are the owners of the hotels that were unknowingly involved in the credit card scam." James took Jordan's arm and escorted her down one side of the long conference table. Kate motioned to Milo to follow her down the other side of the table. They met, hugged and shook hands with everyone in the room. Neither Milo nor Jordan was ready for this kind of greeting, but inside, they were ecstatic!

When they finished meeting everyone, Milo looked at the assembly. "Thank you for appreciating the job we did. We're glad we could help." Jordan turned to James. "We want to thank you and Kate for hiring us to investigate this case." One of the gentlemen stood. "Milo, you and Ms. Sutton saved each of us hundreds of thousands, maybe millions of dollars. Not to mention our reputations. All of us are in the process of restoring our good name with our affected clients." Another owner said, "We have a few surprises for you. Can you tell us how you solved all of this?" Milo gave them a short rundown about his app and how they collected the parts of the puzzle. He mentioned that they were targeted by the people behind this and that Jordan was shot twice.

Jordan nodded, "Yes I was shot, and Milo was shot at, but the guy missed him." She moved her arm up and down, "I'm okay, now." James handed Jordan a stack of envelopes. "'I know we're all glad you're feeling better. These are for you." Jordan looked puzzled as she said, "Thank you, what are they?" A lady at the table said, "Just a few gifts from all of us." James smiled, "Jordan, each hotel wants to treat you and Milo to some wonderful vacations." Jordan glanced at the stack of envelopes. "If we vacation this much, we'll never get any cases solved." Everyone in the room laughed at that statement.

Kate added, "Maybe you can just pop in for a weekend from time to time." Milo thought that might work. "Thank you. We'll come see each of you over the next year. How's that?" Everyone agreed and thought that would be great. Milo addressed everyone in the room, "All of the scanners are destroyed, right?" James told Milo and Jordan that Charlie called all the owners and told them to take the scanners off-line. "Every hotel will be making big changes in their Accounting and Internet departments." One man said, "We sent a large box to an electronic waste disposal event at the mall." Several others said they did the same thing. "We're all going to continue to employ CC Repair to maintain our systems." One owner added, "We had to fire a few bartenders who objected to the loss of extra money. Another said, "I think all of us are on the lookout for new General Managers." He stopped and pointed at Milo. "Are you interested in the job?" Milo laughed, and Jordan said, "You better re-think that idea, if you want to stay in business. We're not the GM types." Once again, everyone in the room laughed and applauded. This time it was for Jordan, who took a bow.

Kate told the owners that Sutton and Starr were at the hotel for a wedding. A lady asked, "Are you guys getting married?" Jordan smiled and got a little flushed as she said, "No, it's not our wedding. It's a long-time friend, CR Reid, who assisted us in this case." James quickly stepped in, "Milo, in the envelopes you'll also find a check from each of the hotels. It's just another way to say thank you for your help in this matter." The hotel owners indicated that they had to get back to work. Each stopped to thank and hug Milo and Jordan again as they left the room.

Milo turned to James and Kate. "Thank you for setting up this meeting." Kate said, "It wasn't us. When the hotel owners found out you were going to be here in Vegas, they insisted on meeting and thanking both of you. We'll see you later at the chapel. It's going to be a beautiful affair."

Jordan and Milo left the conference room a little dazed, to say the least. "How about a drink?" Jordan took his arm. "It's early, but sure, if you're buying." Milo dragged her into the Dublin Pub and was welcomed by Tim, "Top of the Mornin' to ya!" "Hi Tim, I know it's early, but can we have two of your finest beers?" "Ya sure can, I'll bring 'em over, and remember, it's never too early for the world's best beer." They took a table in the corner and Milo put the stack of envelopes in front of Jordan.

He put his hand on the envelopes, "This is something unexpected, huh?" Tim arrived with their drinks. "This round is on me, to say thanks fur gettin' rid of the scanners." Jordan smiled, "Thank you, Tim." Milo asked if he could call Charlie and ask him to drop by. "Sure, I can do that. By the way, everyone in the hotel is gettin' a slight raise, so nobody will be missin' the so-called extra money." Jordan smiled at the tall Irish gent. "I'm glad to hear that." Tim went back to work and Jordan opened the first envelope. She withdrew and opened a short letter. "This is from the Tropics West Hotel. We can stay there a week anytime. There's also a cashier's check." She handed the check to Milo. "It's one-hundred-thousand-dollars?" Jordan opened a second envelope and found another check for the same amount.

"Here's another hundred. She looked in the other four envelopes and found a check in each for the same amount. The last envelope was from James and Kate. She read the note and didn't believe what she saw. "Here, look at this." Milo read the note and then took a big drink of beer. "I can't believe it. They're giving us money and an account at this hotel that we can access anytime? How much money did we get altogether?" Milo took another big drink of his beer while Jordan put all the checks together. "I count six-hundred-thousand plus all the free hotel stays." She clinked her glass with Milo as Charlie entered.

Jordan put all the checks in her purse. Charlie was glad to see them and very happy that the scanners were gone. "Did you catch everyone involved?" Milo told him they did. "All the hotel owners are glad the scanners are gone." Charlie asked, "Can I buy you folks a drink?" They told him one was enough this early in the day. Charlie had an idea. "They should all give you something for making that crap disappear. Maybe a statue." Milo laughed. "Yes, that would be great, a statue of us next to that diamond-shaped Las Vegas sign." Jordan told him they were here for a wedding. "You guys?" "No. Remember CR the FBI agent? He's getting married here, tomorrow." Charlie got beeped on his phone. "Must be trouble somewhere, gotta run. Great seeing you folks, tell CR congratulations for me."

They left Tim a sizable tip and exited the pub smiling and walking around the casino sort of in a daze. Milo said, "Six-hundred grand and a bunch of vacations, I don't believe it." Jordan took his arm and said, "And a statue of us. I know you like that part best." They stopped at the lobby bar. "I lied it's not too early for another drink." He ordered a Mai Tai for each of them, as they stood listening to the sounds of the Vegas slots. Milo had just taken the first sip of his drink when Jordan grabbed his hand. "Where are you dragging me?" "Bring your drink and follow me. She headed them toward the elevators. Moments later they were in their suite. Jordan put the checks and letters on the bar and smiled a lot as she sat on the bed finishing her Mai Tai. "We don't have to get dressed for the wedding and reception dinner for a while so?" She patted the bed and smiled at Milo. He finally got the message and joined her on the bed. He kissed her passionately and then stopped.

Milo jogged to the entry door and hung the do not disturb sign on the handle. Now, nobody would bother them for any reason. He joined Jordan and asked, "How much time do we have?" She began to unbutton her blouse as she answered, "At least an hour. Can you go that long?" Milo rolled to his partner, kissed her again and whispered. "I can! What about you?"

A little over an hour later Milo was sitting against the headboard wishing he had never quit smoking years ago. He was thinking, "*After a session like that, I need a cigarette!*" As Jordan began her shower symphony he walked slowly to the bar and poured himself a glass of beer. He stood staring at the checks and couldn't believe their good fortune. "I still don't believe what we got from this case." Jordan was towel-drying her hair and didn't hear him. "Your turn in the shower." Milo kissed her on the cheek. "Thanks for the daytime fun."

The Orchid Chapel was a perfect location for the late afternoon wedding. Kate and her staff took care of everything. The bride and groom were nervous but were able to get through the ceremony without a hitch. Such was not the case with Jordan, who brought an entire pack of Kleenex in her handbag. Between her and Carol they used almost every single sheet. During the ceremony, Carol noticed that Jordan was holding Milo's hand, and she thought that was sweet. Everyone agreed that it was a beautiful affair.

The reception was also top-notch with great food and music. During the dessert course, Milo took a moment to make a short speech. He congratulated his long-time friend with some light-hearted words and a toast. He asked Jordan to finish his thoughts. She told Mr. and Mrs. Reid that she and Milo had a special gift for them. She smiled as Milo handed the trip planner to CR who opened the packet. "Oh, this is fantastic! Where are we going?" Jordan explained, "It's a first-class all-expense paid honeymoon trip to any destination of your choice." Milo interjected, "Any destination on this planet, you can't go to Mars." Jordan regained control of the hand mic, "You can activate it just by calling our travel agent." CR was very happy with the gift. "Can we go anytime?" Jordan said, "Sure! Have fun."

Milo took James aside and thanked him again for putting the morning meeting together, for the checks, the wedding and the generous invitations to visit their hotels at a future time. James called Kate and Jordan over. "Milo was thanking me for everything that happened during this trip, and I wanted him to know that it was my dear wife who got everything together. She also took care of the wedding." Jordan hugged and thanked Kate who said, "Milo, you know it's always the lady who gets things done." He laughed, but deep inside he knew she was right.

CHAPTER 35

Back Home

Sutton and Starr tried to hit the ground running when they got back to town, but things were piled up too high. Milo was checking a massive amount of email while Carol downloaded and printed out a very long call list from their answering service. She handed the stack of papers to Jordan who sat and began to look them over. "I'm going to need a gallon of coffee to get through this." Milo said, "I need a gallon too. There are way too many emails." Carol headed to the coffee maker, "Don't worry, I can take a hint."

Milo yelled, "Carol, didn't we have a note on the website that said we were out of the office?" She yelled back, "Yes, but some people don't look at the website." She entered the office with a bag of coffee. "I'll bet a lot of the calls came from people who read or saw one of your interviews." Milo thought about it, "You're right. I guess we just can't take off." Jordan looked up from the call list. Carol reminded them, "I always have the calls forwarded to my home phone, but this time, we were all out of town together. I loved the trip, by the way, and didn't want it to end." She went back to the coffee machine.

Their main computer beeped, announcing another email. "It's from James and Kate. They want to make sure we send them an invoice." Jordan couldn't believe it. "What? They want an invoice, after what they did for us? What should we do?" Milo had no idea. "Let me think about it." Jordan reminded him that they needed to go to the bank and deposit the hotel checks. "Should we put them in a savings account?" Milo thought that was best for now and asked, "Do you think we should give Carol a bonus?" She thought for a moment, "Yes, but let's wait for a special occasion."

Milo yawned and agreed. "I'm really tired." Jordan admitted that she was tired too. "I think we need a vacation after our vacation." Carol laughed as she entered with the coffee. I know what you mean. I was up late every night we were at the hotel. There's so much to do." Milo thanked her for the coffee. "Do you ladies think we should take off on a proper vacation?" Jordan looked at Carol and raised her eyebrows. "Do you really think we can do that?" Milo told them that they might be able to get away once they dealt with all the current calls and email messages. Carol asked if it would be a paid vacation. Jordan raised her mug to Carol. "Yes, it will be, for sure." She smiled at Milo and whispered. "That sounds like a special occasion."

Every day the calls kept coming. There were new client meetings daily. S & S found themselves on stakeouts too many nights. Sure, they were busy and were making lots of money, but they almost never got to see each other. Jordan sent a text. *"Milo, meet me at Margo-Rita's at 6."* He smiled and sent back, *"See you there!"* Carol, I'm going out to take a lunch meeting and then I'm going to meet Jordan. Why don't you take off? Put everything on the service. I'll see you tomorrow." Carol loved leaving early. "See you tomorrow boss."

Milo's lunch meeting, with a disgruntled husband, sounded like a million other client meetings he had over the years. He listened to the all too familiar facts, and was about to say no, when the gentleman told him he thought his wife was having an affair with his secretary, Marsha. Milo suddenly perked right up and was all ears. He got the new client's information and told him that he would get back to him as soon as he ran the case by his partner.

It was a little before six when Milo arrived at his favorite casual bar, Margo-Rita's. He scooped up a handful of peanuts from the old barrel near the door as he entered. Margo saw him and came running over. The playful owner hugged and kissed him on the cheek. "Where you been? What about your lady? Did you split up?" "No, we didn't. We've been super busy, and Jordan will be along in a few minutes." She hugged him again, "It's good to see you. Beer?" He said yes and took a seat at their favorite table. He checked his phone for messages and stopped when his beer arrived. Margo took a seat at the table.

"I haven't seen you guys since you solved that big murder case. Where you been?" Milo took a sip of his ice-cold brew. "We've been working on another big case in Las Vegas." Margo said, "I love Las Vegas." She went on and on about Sin City, as she called it. "What is your favorite hotel?" Milo mentioned The Golden Oasis but that's all he got to say because Jordan floated in the front door. Margo saw her and said, "Here's your lady. I'll get her a beer." Milo stood and welcomed his partner with a hug and kiss. Then she saw the lipstick on his cheek. Margo yelled from the bar, "He doesn't have another girlfriend, I kissed him." Jordan smiled and gave him a peck on the other cheek.

The partners sat talking about their day and wondering when they would get back to normal. Milo finished his beer and raised his empty glass. Margo saw his request and asked if they wanted a snack. Jordan asked for onion rings and another beer. Milo took Jordan's hand and wondered if she would like to use one of their free Las Vegas vacations? She thought that might be possible after they wrapped up a few things. Margo set their beer and onion rings on the table. "Enjoy."

Jordan picked up an onion ring and held it like a life preserver. "I want to take a cruise." Milo was super happy to hear that. "Wow, I love the idea. Have you been looking at my email?" Jordan took a bite of the delicious ring, "No, why do you ask?" Milo opened the email on his phone and retrieved an attachment. "Here. Look at this." Jordan glanced quickly at the poster. "Is this what you had in mind? You want us to attend a Private Investigators Conference with guest speakers, forums on new surveillance techniques, concepts for creative bookkeeping and much, much more?" She put the phone down. "Sorry, but that's not my idea of a vacation. Where is this happening?" Milo told her to scroll down below the poster. She looked at the phone again.

"Oh, it's a Hawaiian cruise." Milo pointed to the poster. "The cruise starts and ends in Waikiki." She scrunched up her face, "Well that's different. I like the Hawaii part but not the convention part. If we're going to Hawaii I won't be attending a boring conference. I just want to sit on the sand wearing my bikini with a Mai Tai in my hand. I want to watch the waves, work on my tan and relax."

"Okay, so you're interested in going to Hawaii, but not attending the convention?" Jordan mentioned that she'd never been to the islands but going there was always on her bucket list. Milo looked at his phone again. "The convention organizers sent us a follow-up note asking if we would like to be guest speakers at the convention." Jordan was thinking it over and was just about to say no when Milo read the details. "They'll fly us round trip first class and put us up in a swanky hotel for three days before the cruise and a week after." He was waiting for her reaction. When he didn't get any, he finished reading the details.

"They'll also include a rental car, a food allowance and pay each of us one-thousand dollars for speaking, and we'll have a suite on the ship. Now, what do you say?" Jordan took a sip of her beer. "How many speeches do we have to make during the cruise?" Milo checked the email. "Looks like, just two." She raised a glass to Milo, "That's five-hundred each per speech. I like the payout." Milo finished his beer and asked, "Well?" She looked at him, picked up an onion ring peeked through the center and said. "Aloha! Tell me when to start packing?"

CHAPTER 36

Off to Paradise

Milo's suitcase was twenty pounds under the limit. Jordan's on the other hand, was nine pounds over; she always packed way too much stuff. Their flight to Hawaii was wonderful. They loved the island music during boarding and the first-class service was fantastic. The cabin crew handed each of them an ice-cold glass of guava juice along with a warm, "Aloha, welcome aboard." They received a text from Carol wishing them bon-voyage and thanking them for the unexpected super-large bonus. Everything about the flight made them feel that they were already on vacation in the land of endless summers. Milo was about to turn off his phone when another text arrived. He showed the screen to Jordan. *"Milo & Jordan greetings from the Cook Islands. We LOVE it here! It's the perfect honeymoon destination. Hugs to you both. Mr. & Mrs. CR Reid."* Milo turned off the phone and said, "Cook Islands? I wonder what that cost us? Jordan put her head back in the super-soft seat and told Milo, "It didn't cost me anything. It was charged to your credit card." Milo laughed, and decided to forget all about their business as he sat back and asked for a gin and tonic. They watched an in-flight movie and had a great gourmet lunch. Jordan felt the only thing missing was a foot rub which Milo told her would have to wait till later.

Sutton and Starr were met at Honolulu International Airport with a lei greeting and a limo driver who took them to their five-star hotel right on Waikiki Beach. Jordan picked up several magazines describing scenic sites, attractions and shopping! She kept looking and telling Milo they had to do this and that. They both loved the weather and the palm trees which lined the driveway of the hotel. Just like Las Vegas, the limo driver gave them his card and said, "If you need to go anywhere, just call me." They thanked him as a hotel porter attended to their luggage. The company hosting the cruise had arranged everything for them, so check-in was a breeze.

They entered their spacious suite and the bellman asked if they would like him to open the shutters. The answer was yes. Milo tipped the porter as Jordan stood awestruck by the colors of the water as it lapped up on the beach. "What time are we meeting the organizers of the cruise?" Milo checked the schedule on his cell phone. "Six PM for a meet and greet with drinks." Jordan smiled, "Great, then I have lots of time to put on my bikini and head to the beach. She opened her suitcase and began to look for her swimsuit. Milo started laughing at the pile of clothes she was unearthing to find her skimpy swim togs. "Why did you pack a heavy jacket?" She just glared at him.

Jordan found everything she needed and headed to the bathroom to change. "I brought it because I've never been here, and didn't believe all the weather reports." Milo laughed and took up residence in a very comfortable chair on their lanai overlooking the white sandy beach. A few minutes later, she emerged from the bathroom and asked, "Well, how do I look?" Milo knew there was only one right answer to that question, so he said, "Fantastic. Did you bring sunscreen?" She started looking in her bag as she told him, "I'm glad we came on this trip. This is really special, and I've checked off one thing on my bucket list and no, I didn't bring sunscreen." The hotel's gift shop was their first stop on the way to the beach. Milo applied the SPF 30 spray to his partner and found a comfortable spot to watch her play mermaid. It wasn't long before the island temperature and soft breeze made him forget about work and relax for the first time in a long time.

Jordan had fun splashing around in the warm Hawaiian waters and had to laugh as she approached her sleeping partner. She nudged him, and he asked the same question she always asked, "Was I sleeping?" She laughed and dragged him up. "We have to get going. We're meeting and greeting people today, and we have to look nice." She kissed her guy and told him to get dressed early. "We should walk around this beautiful area before meeting with the organizers for sunset drinks and dinner." That's exactly what they did. For several hours they were just two tourists wandering all over Waikiki looking and taking photos of everything. It was getting close to six o'clock when they located the hotel bar where the opening night party was taking place. They approached the sign-in table, presented their business card and the head greeter welcomed both of them with a beautiful flower lei and a kiss on the cheek. The organizers, who were excited to have such "superstars" attending their event, introduced S & S to everyone. They met Investigators from many states, Canada and England. Milo didn't remember many, if any, of the names because of the strong drinks and the wonderful appetizers.

They all stood together watching the spectacular Hawaiian sunset. Jordan loved the party and the location. She wondered what time they needed to be at the dock to board the ship. One of the cruise directors explained the schedule, "The ship sails at seven PM, but everyone can get onboard as early as noon." Milo wondered what they had planned for the first day. The young cruise organizer said, "You board early, check out the ship, eat lunch, have a few drinks and get ready for the sail-away party. Here's your schedule for the conference." Jordan looked at the several pages and realized that they really would be speaking only twice. "That's great." Milo agreed, "Since the ship docks on three islands and the speeches take place while we're at sea, I guess we'll have time to see some of the sights."

They used their pre-cruise free time wisely and took a few sightseeing tours on Oahu. Saturday was boarding day. The limo driver picked them up at the hotel and escorted S & S to the dock. They were excited as they checked-in and boarded the ship. Their luggage was already in their balcony stateroom, so they decided to walk around to get acquainted with everything. They felt like such country bumpkins, because they didn't know which way was forward or aft. "We'll laugh about this in days to come." Milo said, "Let's just not tell anybody we got lost." They finally found the theatre and ran into one of the conference organizers. "This is where you'll be speaking." Milo thanked the gentleman for the information, "Now, if we can only find it again."

When the ship docked on Maui, S & S took off to explore the Valley Island because their first speech wasn't scheduled until the following afternoon when they would be at sea heading to island of Hawaii. They took a guided tour because they figured if they couldn't find their way around the ship, they'd never make it trying to see Maui. They had a wonderful day in the warm Hawaiian sun. Jordan got a little burnt but not bad. They had a great dinner with their new convention friends. Milo lost the coin toss and had to speak first. It was a double loss as he also had to massage Jordan's feet. He liked that part because it meant a night of hugs and kisses at sea.

The next afternoon, as the ship sailed away from Maui, it was time for Milo's speech. After he thanked everyone for attending he really didn't know what to say to this distinguished gathering of Investigators, so he just opened the floor to questions. A few hands raised asking, "How long have you been in business? How did you meet Jordan? How many cases do you have open at this time and where do you advertise for business?" He told them about meeting Jordan in college. "She went into the Police Academy, and I became one of you." He then talked briefly about why Jordan quit the police department and came to work with him. He answered as many questions as he could in the time allotted. "We'll be around every day so, if you have more questions, please ask. The moderator said that Jordan would be speaking in two days as they were sailing from Kona to the island of Kaua'i. The theatre cleared, and Jordan looked at Milo. "Well, you just did my entire speech. What am I going to talk about?" Milo apologized and offered a solution. "Why don't you do the same thing I did. Just open the floor to questions and see what happens. I'll be with you so if there are no questions, I'll jump in." She said, "Okay, but I think you owe me another foot rub tonight for stealing my speech." Milo smiled and begrudgingly agreed.

Jordan started her talk with a short bio and then asked for questions. Unlike Milo's speech, where only five hands were raised, almost every hand in the theatre went up. She looked over at Milo and grinned as she said, "I got this." She did extremely well and received a standing ovation. They both took bows. Jordan told everyone if they had additional questions, they would be around.

On their final night at sea, the organizers asked if Milo and Jordan would do one more Q & A session for everybody. "I know we asked for two speeches, but everyone has more to ask." Jordan said, "Sure, we'd love to." A little later, they entered the theatre and saw two armchairs on stage. Milo and Jordan were escorted to the stage and took their seats. Milo quipped, "I assume these are for us?" An audience member asked once again about advertising. Milo told him they weren't doing ads right now. "I used to buy phone book ads when I first started, but right now, since we've been on TV and in countless news stories we don't have to."

Jordan added, "Milo never mentioned this, but we have a biographer. We met a writer named J.E. Duke, who has chronicled several of our cases and said he'd like to continue if it's alright with us." That comment brought on another series of questions about the stories. Jordan answered, "He wrote about the first time Milo and I hooked up." Milo smiled and looked away. "It was a spicy night for sure and you can read about it in his book, "She Works with Killers." Milo said, "That title tells it all, because that's how we met—she was working with a bunch of killers and didn't know it." Jordan said the writer also chronicled their case where they came face-to-face with the world's most wanted Assassin named Whisper. Milo added, "It's just like Doctor John Watson writing about Sherlock Holmes." Everyone laughed. Jordan said, "Except you don't smoke a pipe or wear a deerstalker hat." That brought on another round of laughter.

The Q & A session concluded late with the organizers thanking Sutton and Starr and inviting everyone to the Aft Bar for a final drink to close out the night. The questions continued long into the night and S & S didn't mind because they had a great time and didn't want the cruise to end. But it did end as they docked back in Honolulu at seven the next morning. Before they left the ship, they were invited to a luau that evening. They were dressed and ready at four PM for the pick-up. It was a wonderful way to end their week of fun at sea. Milo ate and drank way too much; he even got up and shook his hips with the beautiful

Tahitian dancers. Jordan recorded his "actions" on her phone and would make sure Carol saw it upon their return.

Following their fantastic island cruise, Sutton and Starr spent a second week in another Waikiki beach-front hotel. They had a wonderful, relaxing time in Hawaii and returned home rejuvenated and ready for whatever lay ahead of them. They learned that aloha means hello and goodbye, but most of all

"Aloha means LOVE"

About the Author

(J.E. Duke - A.K.A. Aloha JOE®)

J.E. Duke is an Emmy Award-winning writer/producer who has worked in all phases of the entertainment industry. **"Million Dollar Fraud"** is his sixth offering to the world of fiction.

Aloha JOE®, a Hawaiian radio broadcaster and music producer began sending "The Music & Spirit of Hawaii" worldwide in 1994.

Also by J.E. Duke

"Million Dollar Fraud"
A Sutton & Starr Mystery (Book 3)

"Honorable Assassin"
A Sutton & Starr Mystery (Book 2)

"She Works with Killers"
A Sutton & Starr Mystery (Book 1)

"Never Too Late for Love"
Contemporary Romance

*"Family Lies: Generations of Deceit"
A Romantic Mystery

*NOTE

The characters James and Kate Forbes featured in Million-Dollar Fraud were introduced in Family Lies - Generations of Deceit.

Read the synopsis at www.jeduke.com

All books are available as digital novels and in paperback form at many online retailers.

Visit the author's website - **www.jeduke.com**